READ & LISTEN OS MELHORES CONTOS DO SÉCULO XX EM VERSÃO ORIGINAL NA ÍNTEGRA

"Sometimes all we need is a fine, short story."

Martins Fontes

Salman Rushdie
The Courter

•

Philip Roth
Defender of the Faith

© 1994 por Salman Rushdie. The Wylie Agency, Ltd., UK.
© 1959, 1964, 1987 por Philip Roth. The Wylie Agency, Ltd., UK.
© 2011 Martins Editora Livraria Ltda., São Paulo, para a presente edição.

Publisher	*Evandro Mendonça Martins Fontes*
Coordenação editorial	*Anna Dantes*
Produção editorial	*Alyne Azuma*
Tradução	*Betty Nisembaum*
Revisão	*André Albert*
	Denise Roberti Camargo
	Dinarte Zorzanelli da Silva
Biografias e apresentações	*Laura Fernández*
Locução de "The Courter"	*Julian Jahanpour*
Locução de "Defender of the Faith"	*David Tamke*
Gravação	*RecLab*
Técnico	*Francesc Gosalves*

Dados Internacionais de Catalogação na Publicação (CIP)
(Câmara Brasileira do Livro, SP, Brasil)

Rushdie, Salman, 1947-.
 The courter / Salman Rushdie. Defender of the faith / Philip Roth / [tradução Betty Nisembaum]. – 1. ed.– São Paulo : Martins Martins Fontes, 2011.

 Título original: The courter ; Defender of the faith.
 Inclui CD.
 ISBN 978-85-8063-011-4

 1. Contos indianos (Inglês) 2. Contos norte-americanos I. Roth, Philip, 1933-. II. Título. III. Título: Defender of the faith.

11-02233   CDD-823
                                                                              -813

Índices para catálogo sistemático:
 1. Contos : Literatura indiana em inglês   823
 2. Contos : Literatura norte-americana   813

Todos os direitos desta edição para o Brasil reservados à
Martins Editora Livraria Ltda.
Av. Dr. Arnaldo, 2076
01255-000 São Paulo SP Brasil
Tel. (11) 3116.0000
info@martinseditora.com.br
www.martinsmartinsfontes.com.br

SUMÁRIO

INTRODUÇÃO 9

Salman Rushdie
BIOGRAFIA 13
APRESENTAÇÃO DO CONTO 15
The Courter 17

Philip Roth
BIOGRAFIA 57
APRESENTAÇÃO DO CONTO 59
Defender of the Faith 61

INTRODUÇÃO
Dê um passo além e leia os clássicos em versão original

Para muitos de nós, ler em versão original supõe um desafio por vezes irrealizável. Habituados a nossa própria língua, ficamos frustrados quando não entendemos todas as palavras de um texto. Quantas vezes deixamos um livro de lado porque não queremos consultar o dicionário a toda hora? Essa consulta (quase sempre obrigatória) se soma ao desconhecimento das referências culturais, à dificuldade de perceber os matizes, a ironia do autor etc. Logo nos aborrecemos por não conseguir compreender a essência do relato e acabamos fechando o livro e buscando a versão traduzida.

Na coleção READ & LISTEN a leitura e audição do texto original produzem experiências tão únicas quanto a de contemplar uma pintura em vez de sua reprodução. Não só se aprende como também se desfruta e assimila o verdadeiro espírito do relato.

Aqui, os leitores podem ter acesso aos melhores contos dos mais respeitados autores de língua inglesa, com as ferramentas necessárias para compreender os textos em sua totalidade.

Foi-se o tempo de ler com o dicionário do lado. Cada conto inclui um extenso glossário para que não seja necessário interromper a leitura. Além de todas as palavras que você pode não entender, ele apresenta referências culturais, deixa claras as nuances e permite compreender todos os toques irônicos de cada conto. Para quem quer praticar a compreensão oral ou simplesmente ouvir o texto enquanto o lê, nada mais simples. Ponha o CD com a versão em áudio dos contos para tocar, sente-se, relaxe e deixe que um locutor nativo conte a história. Porque não há maneira melhor de colocar ao seu alcance essas obras-primas do que rompendo as barreiras que o mantiveram longe delas durante tanto tempo.

Quem tem medo dos clássicos?

E por falar em clássicos... Nossa seleção se guiou por várias premissas: em primeiro lugar, os contos tinham de ser sugestivos e não muito complexos; em segundo lugar, tinham de representar o mundo próprio de cada autor. Clássicos em miniatura, inesquecíveis, os contos desta coleção devem ser lidos com cuidado, degustando cada frase, cada palavra. São obras capazes de transformar seus personagens em alguém conhecido, quase familiar, que poderia ser seu melhor amigo.

Acreditamos que, depois de tanto tempo aprendendo inglês, chegou seu momento de desfrutar. Você merece.

Salman Rushdie
The Courter

"On the radio, people were always singing about the joys of being sixteen years old. I wondered where they were, all those boys and girls of my age having the time of their lives."

BIOGRAFIA
Salman Rushdie

Quando pequeno, ele queria ser ator. Uma estrela de Hollywood. Ainda hoje assegura que, se não tivesse ido parar na literatura, poderia ter ganhado um Oscar. *Sir* Ahmed Salman Rushdie (Mumbai, 1947) não é só o autor perseguido de *Os versos satânicos*, mas também um autêntico *showman*, viciado na literatura sinuosa de Thomas Pynchon. Independente de pesarem sobre ele uma condenação à morte (o aiatolá Ruholá Khomeini, líder religioso do Irã, a emitiu em 1989 e, como faleceu pouco depois, não pôde revogá-la; portanto, ela continua vigente) e uma séria ameaça da Al-Qaeda (que não viu com bons olhos a nomeação dele a Cavaleiro do Império Britânico em 2007), o escritor não perdeu o senso de humor. Quando lhe perguntaram o que fazia saindo com uma jovem modelo, ele respondeu: "Me cansam as pessoas que só falam de literatura".

Rushdie tinha 14 anos quando seus pais, um rico empresário indiano e uma professora, o mandaram ao Reino Unido para estudar. Matriculou-se na Rugby School, um dos internatos de maior prestígio do país, e passou maus bocados porque era motivo de gozação de seus companheiros. Riam da sua origem indiana e de como jogava mal futebol.

Em 1968 obteve seu doutorado em História na prestigiosa Universidade de Cambridge, e sete anos depois, em 1975, publicou seu primeiro romance, *Grimus*, uma história de ficção científica completamente ignorada tanto pela crítica como pelo público.

Mas se dedicou a fundo, e o segundo, *Os filhos da meia-noite*, conseguiu o prestigioso Booker Prize em 1981. Rushdie abandonou a ficção científica e se especializou em uma espécie de realismo mágico oriental, que colocou à disposição da força motriz de sua literatura: o choque entre Oriente e Ocidente. A história de Saleem Sinai, o protagonista de *Os filhos da meia-noite*, é a colisão entre dois mundos condenados a entender-se, porém incapazes de se olhar nos olhos. Esse é o motor também de "The Courter" e de boa parte da sua narrativa.

Sua complicada vida sentimental merece uma menção à parte. Rushdie se casou pela primeira vez em 1976 com Clarissa Luard, com quem teve um filho (Zafer), e se divorciou seis anos após ganhar o Booker, em 1987. Pouco depois, conquistou a escritora Marianne Wiggins, com quem foi casado entre 1988 e 1993. Passou quatro anos solteiro e, quando fez 50 anos, casou-se com Elizabeth West. Divorciaram-se em 2004. Eles têm um filho, Milan. No mesmo ano do divórcio, Rushdie pediu em casamento a modelo Padma Lakshmi. A relação durou até 2007. Um ano depois, completados 61 anos de idade, o escritor caiu nos braços de outra modelo indiana, Riya Sen.

Rushdie não conseguiu esquecer sua paixão pelo cinema. Por isso, faz figurações relâmpago em filmes de todos os tipos (*O diário de Bridget Jones*, por exemplo) e no videoclipe de "*The Ground Beneath Her Feet*", do U2 – canção, aliás, baseada no livro de mesmo título do escritor. Apesar de sua produção ser ampla e diversa, *Os versos satânicos* continua sendo sua obra mais conhecida, acima de tudo pela tragédia que a rodeia, uma vez que provocou não só a queima de livrarias, como também a morte de ao menos 38 pessoas (seu tradutor para o japonês e as 37 pessoas que se encontravam num hotel de Sivas, na Turquia, quando os violentos manifestantes contra seu tradutor para o turco assaltaram o local), e eclipsou uma importante produção de contos, cujo expoente máximo é a antologia *Oriente, Ocidente* (1994), na qual se inclui "The Courter".

LAURA FERNÁNDEZ

APRESENTAÇÃO DO CONTO
The Courter

É verão em Londres, o verão de Sam Cooke, e estamos no início dos anos 1960. É o verão de Sam Cooke porque Sam Cooke é só o que escutam no prédio de apartamentos em que vivem um jovem de origem indiana e sua família. O prédio é vigiado por um porteiro também de origem hindu, que mal sabe falar inglês. A babá da família, que acaba de se mudar para Waverly House (nome do edifício em questão), o chama de *courter* por ter um problema com a letra "p" e ser incapaz de dizer *porter* ("porteiro", em inglês). A babá, que todos chamam de Certainly-Mary (Certamente-Mary, em tradução literal, porque tudo para ela é "certamente sim" ou "certamente não"), é tão pequena que os degraus do Waverly House lhe parecem os Alpes.

Certainly-Mary sai com Mixed-Up (é assim que os jovens chamam o porteiro), que fala um inglês tão ruim quanto o do pai do protagonista (as confusões e embaraços são constantes). Roy Orbison canta "It's Over" e The Four Seasons entoam "Sherry" – os anos 1960 estão em toda parte, e, para o protagonista, ter dezesseis anos é o pior que pode acontecer a uma pessoa.

Incluído na célebre antologia *Oriente, Ocidente*, publicada em 1994 (cinco anos após ter estourado o escândalo de *Os versos satânicos*), "The Courter" é o conto que encerra a compilação, dividida em três partes: Leste, Oeste e Leste/Oeste. É também um dos que melhor resume a força motriz da narrativa de Rushdie: o choque entre Oriente e Ocidente, o cruzamento de culturas, a identidade difusa daquele que cruza a fronteira – essa fronteira invisível que existe entre "nós" e "os outros". O protagonista não é, como Saleem Sinai, a criança enigmática de *Os filhos da meia-noite*, um rapaz jovem com superpoderes, e sim um jovem qualquer que aprende a falar inglês no ritmo dos *Beatles*, que zomba de sua babá (personagem emotiva e heroica) por ela não conseguir dizer "porter" e do porteiro (um autêntico superdotado, fechado em sua cabeça), porque este enrola as frases. Um jovem que, como o próprio Rushdie, cresceu enfrentando como pôde o fato de ser diferente. "The Courter" é, definitivamente, uma fábula moderna de um dos melhores escritores do século sobre a dificuldade de encaixar-se em um mundo em que tudo já está pressuposto.

No que tange ao estritamente formal, o conto está construído como um quebra-cabeça. A compreensão está garantida graças à ajuda de um glossário que acompanha cada página desta edição, e a leitura é mais saborosa do que nunca. É que, sem a ajuda de um contexto e sem entender as nuances de cada palavra dita pelos protagonistas, o conto seria difícil de entender para alguém que não esteja familiarizado com as culturas indiana e inglesa. Uma vez superado o medo de enfrentar o texto, cada nova intervenção de Certainly-Mary ou do porteiro é hilária. Sem dúvida, algo que deve ser apreciado em versão original. E se alguém pudesse contar essa história, como de fato o faz o protagonista, a partir das últimas notícias que tem de sua babá até... até onde? Não revelaremos nada, mas você pode escutar a versão em áudio, que permite, entre outras coisas, dar uma espiada (na realidade uma "escutada") no estranho sotaque da senhorita Certainly-Mary.

LAURA FERNÁNDEZ

The Courter

1

CERTAINLY-MARY WAS THE SMALLEST woman Mixed-Up the hall porter[1] had come across, dwarfs[2] excepted, a tiny sixty-year-old Indian lady with her greying hair[3] tied behind her head in a neat bun[4], hitching up her red-hemmed white sari[5] in the front and negotiating the apartment block's front steps as if they were Alps. 'No,' he said aloud, furrowing his brow[6]. What would be the right peaks[7]. Ah, good, that was the name. 'Ghats[8],' he said proudly. Word from a schoolboy atlas long ago, when India felt as far away as Paradise. (Nowadays Paradise seemed even further away but India, and Hell, had come a good bit closer.) 'Western Ghats, Eastern Ghats, and now Kensington[9] Ghats,' he said, giggling[10]. 'Mountains.'

She stopped in front of him in the oak-panelled lobby[11]. 'But ghats in India are also stairs,' she said. 'Yes yes certainly. For instance in Hindu holy city of Varanasi[12], where the Brahmins[13] sit taking the filgrims'[14] money is called Dasashwamedh-ghat. Broad-broad staircase down to River Ganga[15]. O, most certainly! Also Manikarnika-ghat. They buy fire

---

1 **hall porter:** porteiro • 2 **dwarfs:** anões • 3 **greying hair:** cabelo ficando grisalho • 4 **a neat bun:** um coque impecável • 5 **hitching up her red-hemmed sari:** puxando seu sári de bainha vermelha • 6 **furrowing his brow:** afundando sua sobrancelha • 7 **peaks:** picos • 8 **Ghats:** cadeias de montanhas da Índia • 9 **Kensington:** um bom bairro de Londres • 10 **giggling:** com uma risadinha • 11 **oak-panelled lobby:** portaria com painéis de carvalho • 12 **Varanasi:** cidade sagrada do hinduísmo • 13 **Brahmin:** brâmane (membros da casta sacerdotal hindu) • 14 **filgrims (pilgrims):** peregrinos • 15 **River Ganga:** rio Ganges

from a house with a tiger leaping[1] from the roof - yes certainly, a statue tiger, coloured by Technicolor, what are you thinking? – and they bring it in a box to set fire[2] to their loved ones' bodies. Funeral fires are of sandal[3]. Photographs not allowed; no, certainly not.'

He began thinking of her as Certainly-Mary because she never said plain yes or no[4]; always this O-yes-certainly or no-certainly-not. In the confused circumstances that had prevailed[5] ever since his brain, his one sure thing, had let him down[6], he could hardly be certain of anything any more; so he was stunned by her sureness[7], first into nostalgia, then envy, then attraction. And attraction was a thing so long forgotten that when the churning[8] started he thought for a long time it must be the Chinese dumplings[9] he had brought home from the High Street carry-out[10].

English was hard for Certainly-Mary, and this was a part of what drew damaged old Mixed-Up towards her[11]. The letter p was a particular problem, often turning into an f or a c; when she proceeded through the lobby with a wheeled wicker shopping basket[12], she would say, 'Going shocking[13],' and when, on her return, he offered to help lift the basket up the

---

1 **leaping:** saltando • 2 **set fire:** atear fogo • 3 **sandal:** sândalo • 4 **plain yes or no:** um simples sim ou não • 5 **had prevailed:** haviam prevalecido • 6 **his brain... had let him down:** seu cérebro o havia deixado na mão • 7 **he was stunned by her sureness:** estava impressionado com a segurança dela • 8 **churning:** agitação • 9 **Chinese dumplings**: bolinho chinês cozido recheado (guioza) • 10 **carry-out:** comida para viagem • 11 **what drew (him) towards her:** o que o atraía nela • 12 **wheeled wicker shopping basket:** carrinho de compra de vime • 13 **going shocking (going shopping):** vou às compras (*shocking* significa "espantoso" ou "escandaloso")

front ghats, she would answer, 'Yes, fleas[1].' As the elevator lifted her away, she called through the grille[2]: 'Oé, courter! Thank you, courter. O, yes, certainly.' (In Hindi and Konkani[3], however, her p's knew their place.)

So: thanks to her unexpected, somehow stomach-churning[4] magic, he was no longer porter, but courter[5]. 'Courter,' he repeated to the mirror when she had gone. His breath[6] made a little dwindling[7] picture of the word on the glass. 'Courter courter caught.' Okay. People called him many things, he did not mind. But this name, this courter, this he would try to be.

2

For years now I've been meaning[8] to write down the story of Certainly-Mary, our ayah[9], the woman who did as much as my mother to raise[10] my sisters and me, and her great adventure with her 'courter' in London, where we all lived for a time in the early Sixties in a block called Waverley House; but what with one thing and another I never got round to it[11].

Then recently I heard from Certainly-Mary after a longish[12] silence. She wrote to say that she was ninety-one, had had a serious operation, and would I kindly send her some money, because she was embarrassed that her niece, with whom she was now living in the Kurla district of Bombay, was so badly out of pocket[13].

---

1 **yes, fleas (yes, please):** sim, por favor (*fleas* são "pulgas") • 2 **grille:** grade • 3 **Konkani:** língua oficial do estado de Goa (Índia) • 4 **stomach-churning:** de dar nó no estômago • 5 **courter:** palavra inventada que deriva do verbo *to court* (cortejar) • 6 **breath:** respiração • 7 **dwindling:** que foi desaparecendo • 8 **I've been meaning:** eu queria • 9 **ayah:** babá • 10 **to raise:** criar • 11 **what with one thing and another I never got round to it:** entre uma coisa e outra nunca encontrei o momento de fazer isso • 12 **longish:** bastante longo • 13 **out of pocket:** sem dinheiro

I sent the money, and soon afterwards received a pleasant letter from the niece, Stella, written in the same hand as the letter from 'Aya' – as we had always called Mary, palindromically dropping the 'h'[1]. Aya had been so touched[2], the niece wrote, that I remembered her after all these years. 'I have been hearing the stories about you folks[3] all my life,' the letter went on, 'and I think of you a little bit as family. Maybe you recall my mother, Mary's sister. She unfortunately passed on[4]. Now it is I who write Mary's letters for her. We all wish you the best.'

This message from an intimate stranger reached out to me[5] in my enforced exile from the beloved[6] country of my birth and moved me, stirring[7] things that had been buried very deep. Of course it also made me feel guilty about having done so little for Mary over the years. For whatever reason, it has become more important than ever to set down the story I've been carrying around unwritten for so long, the story of Aya and the gentle man whom she renamed – with unintentional but prophetic overtones[8] of romance – 'the courter'. I see now that it is not just their story, but ours, mine, as well.

3

His real name was Mecir: you were supposed to say Mishirsh because it had invisible accents on it in some Iron Curtain[9] language in which the accents had to be invisible, my sis-

---

1 **palindromically dropping the 'h':** palindromicamente abrindo mão do "h" (um palíndromo é uma palavra que se lê igual de trás para a frente) • 2 **so touched:** tão emocionada • 3 **you folks:** vocês (coloquial) • 4 **passed on:** faleceu • 5 **reached out to me:** me tocou • 6 **beloved:** amado • 7 **stirring:** despertando; remexendo • 8 **overtones:** nuances • 9 **Iron Curtain:** Cortina de Ferro

ter Durré said solemnly, in case somebody spied on them or rubbed them out[1] or something. His first name also began with an m but it was so full of what we called Communist consonants, all those z's and c's and w's walled up together[2] without vowels to give them breathing space, that I never even tried to learn it.

At first we thought of nicknaming him[3] after a mischievous[4] little comic-book character, Mr Mxyztplk from the Fifth Dimension, who looked a bit like Elmer Fudd[5] and used to make Superman's life hell until ole Supe[6] could trick him into saying[7] his name backwards, Klptzyxm, whereupon he disappeared back into the Fifth Dimension; but because we weren't too sure how to say Mxyztplk (not to mention Klptzyxm) we dropped that idea. 'We'll just call you Mixed-Up,' I told him in the end, to simplify life. 'Mishter Mikshed-Up Mishirsh.' I was fifteen then and bursting with unemployed cock[8] and it meant I could say things like that right into people's faces, even people less accommodating[9] than Mr Mecir with his stroke.

What I remember most vividly are his pink rubber washing-up gloves, which he seemed never to remove, at least not until he came calling for Certainly-Mary...

At any rate, when I insulted him, with my sisters Durré and Muneeza cackling[10] in the lift, Mecir just grinned an empty

---

1 **in case somebody spied on them or rubbed them out:** no caso de alguém espiá-los ou eliminá-los • 2 **walled up together:** emparedadas • 3 **nicknaming him:** apelidando-o • 4 **mischievous:** malicioso • 5 **Elmer Fudd:** Hortelino Troca-Letras (personagem de desenho animado) • 6 **ole Supe:** Super--Homem • 7 **could trick him into saying:** levá-lo a dizer • 8 **bursting with unemployed cock:** explodindo com palavrões contidos • 9 **accommodating:** complacentes • 10 **cackling:** cacarejando

good-natured grin[1], nodded[2], 'You call me what you like, okay,' and went back to buffing and polishing the brasswork[3]. There was no point teasing him[4] if he was going to be like that, so I got into the lift and all the way to the fourth floor we sang *I Can't Stop Loving You* at the top of our best Ray Charles voices, which were pretty awful. But we were wearing our dark glasses, so it didn't matter.

4

It was the summer of 1962, and school was out[5]. My baby sister Scheherazade was just one year old. Durré was a bee-hived[6] fourteen; Muneeza was ten, and already quite a handful[7]. The three of us – or rather Durré and me, with Muneeza trying desperately and unsuccessfully to be included in our gang – would stand over Scheherazade's cot[8] and sing to her. 'No nursery rhymes[9],' Durré had decreed, and so there were none, for though she was a year my junior she was a natural leader. The infant Scheherazade's lullabies[10] were our cover versions of recent hits by Chubby Checker, Neil Sedaka, Elvis and Pat Boone.

'Why don't you come home, Speedy Gonzales?' we bellowed[11] in sweet disharmony: but most of all, and with actions, we would jump down, turn around and pick a bale of

---

1 **good-natured grin:** sorriso bonachão • 2 **nodded:** meneou a cabeça • 3 **went back to buffing and polishing the brasswork:** voltou a limpar e a polir os metais • 4 **there was no point teasing him:** não fazia sentido provocá-lo • 5 **school was out:** eram férias escolares • 6 **beehived:** com o cabelo arrumado em um grande topete • 7 **quite a handful:** dava muito trabalho • 8 **cot:** berço • 9 **no nursery rhymes:** nada de canções de ninar • 10 **lullabies:** canções de ninar • 11 **we bellowed:** berrávamos

cotton[1]. We would have jumped down, turned around and picked those bales all day except that the Maharaja[2] of B— in the flat below complained, and Aya Mary came in to plead with us[3] to be quiet.

'Look, see, it's Jumble-Aya who's fallen for[4] Mixed-Up,' Durré shouted, and Mary blushed a truly immense blush[5]. So naturally we segued right into[6] a 'quick me-oh-my-oh; son of a gun[7], we had big fun. But then the baby began to yell[8], my father came in with his head down bull-fashion and steaming[9] from both ears, and we needed all the good luck charms[10] we could find.

I had been at boarding school[11] in England for a year or so when Abba[12] took the decision to bring the family over[13]. Like all his decisions, it was neither explained to nor discussed with anyone, not even my mother. When they first arrived he rented two adjacent flats in a seedy[14] Bayswater[15] mansion block called Graham Court, which lurked[16] furtively in a nothing street that crawled[17] along the side of the ABC Queensway cinema towards the Porchester Baths. He commandeered[18] one of these flats for himself and put my mother, three sisters and Aya in the other; also, on school holidays, me. England,

---

1 **we would jump down, turn around and pick a bale of cotton:** nós teríamos pulado, dado uma volta e pegado um fardo de algodão (trecho de *Pick a Bale of Cotton* – canção de trabalho do período da escravidão) • 2 **Maharaja:** marajá • 3 **came in to plead with us:** veio nos suplicar • 4 **fallen for:** se apaixonou • 5 **blushed a truly immense blush:** seu rosto ficava extremamente corado • 6 **we segued right into:** em seguida emendávamos com • 7 **son of a gun:** filho da mãe • 8 **to yell:** gritar • 9 **steaming:** soltando fumaça pelas narinas • 10 **good luck charms:** amuletos da sorte • 11 **boarding school:** internato • 12 **Abba:** papai (em híndi) • 13 **to bring the family over:** trazer a família toda • 14 **seedy:** gasta; decadente • 15 **Bayswater:** bairro de Londres • 16 **lurked:** espreitava • 17 **crawled:** serpenteava • 18 **he commandeered:** se apoderou

where liquor was freely available, did little for my father's *bonhomie*[1], so in a way it was a relief[2] to have a flat to ourselves.

Most nights he emptied a bottle of Johnnie Walker Red Label and a soda-siphon. My mother did not dare to[3] go across to 'his place' in the evenings. She said: 'He makes faces at me.'

Aya Mary took Abba his dinner and answered all his calls (if he wanted anything, he would phone us up and ask for it). I am not sure why Mary was spared his drunken rages[4]. She said it was because she was nine years his senior[5], so she could tell him to show due respect.

After a few months, however, my father leased[6] a three-bedroom fourth-floor apartment with a fancy address[7]. This was Waverley House in Kensington Court, W8. Among its other residents were not one but two Indian Maharajas, the sporting Prince P— as well as the old B— who has already been mentioned. Now we were jammed in together[8], my parents and Baby Scare-zade (as her siblings[9] had affectionately begun to call her) in the master bedroom, the three of us in a much smaller room, and Mary, I regret to admit, on a straw mat[10] laid on the fitted carpet[11] in the hall. The third bedroom became my father's office, where he made phone-calls and kept his *Encyclopaedia Britannica,* his *Reader's Digests,* and (under lock and key[12]) the television cabinet[13]. We entered it at our peril[14]. It was the Minotaur's lair[15].

---

1 **bonhomie**: cordialidade; amabilidade • 2 **a relief:** um alívio • 3 **did not dare to:** não se atrevia • 4 **was spared his drunken rages:** era poupada dos seus acessos de raiva devidos à bebida • 5 **nine years his senior:** nove anos mais velha que ele • 6 **leased:** alugou • 7 **a fancy address:** um endereço chique • 8 **jammed in together:** apertados juntos • 9 **siblings:** irmãos • 10 **on a straw mat:** sobre uma esteira de palha • 11 **fitted carpet:** carpete • 12 **under lock and key:** fechado a sete chaves • 13 **cabinet:** armário • 14 **at our peril:** por nossa conta e risco • 15 **lair:** covil

One morning he was persuaded to drop in[1] at the corner pharmacy and pick up some supplies for the baby. When he returned there was a hurt, schoolboyish look on his face that I had never seen before, and he was pressing his hand against his cheek.

'She hit me,' he said plaintively[2].

'Hai! Allah-tobah! Darling!' cried my mother, fussing[3]. 'Who hit you? Are you injured? Show me, let me see.'

'I did nothing,' he said, standing there in the hall with the pharmacy bag in his other hand and a face as pink as Mecir's rubber gloves[4]. 'I just went in with your list. The girl seemed very helpful. I asked for baby compound[5], Johnson's powder[6], teething jelly[7], and she brought them out. Then I asked did she have any nipples[8], and she slapped my face[9].'

My mother was appalled[10]. 'Just for that?' And Certainly-Mary backed her up. 'What is this nonsense?' she wanted to know. 'I have been in that chemist's shock[11], and they have flenty nickels[12], different sizes, all on view.'

Durré and Muneeza could not contain themselves. They were rolling round on the floor[13], laughing and kicking their legs in the air.

'You both shut your face[14] at once,' my mother ordered. 'A madwoman has hit your father. Where is the comedy[15]?'

---

1 **to drop in:** passar por • 2 **plaintively:** queixoso • 3 **fussing:** armando um estardalhaço • 4 **rubber gloves:** luvas de borracha • 5 **baby compound:** pomada para bebês • 6 **powder:** talco • 7 **teething jelly:** pasta de dentes para bebê • 8 **nipples:** mamilos • 9 **she slapped my face:** me deu um tapa no rosto • 10 **appalled:** horrorizada • 11 **chemist's shock (chemist's shop):** farmácia (*shock* significa "susto") • 12 **flenty nickles (plenty of nipples):** muitos bicos (*nickles* são "moedas de cinco centavos") • 13 **rolling around on the floor:** rolavam no chão • 14 **shut your face:** calem-se • 15 **where is the comedy?:** qual é a graça?

'I don't believe it,' Durré gasped[1]. 'You just went up to that girl and said,' and here she fell apart again[2], stamping her feet[3] and holding her stomach, ' "*have you got any nipples?*" '

My father grew thunderous, empurpled[4]. Durré controlled herself. 'But Abba,' she said, at length, 'here they call them teats[5].'

Now my mother's and Mary's hands flew to their mouths, and even my father looked shocked. 'But how shameless[6]!' my mother said. 'The same word as for what's on your bosoms[7]?' She coloured, and stuck out her tongue for shame[8].

'These English,' sighed Certainly-Mary. 'But aren't they the limit[9]?Certainly-yes; they are.'

I remember this story with delight, because it was the only time I ever saw my father so discomfited[10], and the incident became legendary and the girl in the pharmacy was installed as the object of our great veneration. (Durré and I went in there just to take a look at her – she was a plain, short girl of about seventeen, with large, unavoidable breasts[11] – but she caught us whispering and glared so fiercely that we fled[12].) And also because in the general hilarity I was able to conceal[13] the shaming truth that I, who had been in England for so long, would have made the same mistake as Abba did.

---

1 **gasped:** disse engasgando • 2 **she fell apart again:** voltou a rir descontroladamente • 3 **stamping her feet:** batendo os pés no chão • 4 **grew thunderous, empurpled:** ficou furioso, colérico • 5 **teats:** bico de mamadeira • 6 **shameless:** sem vergonha • 7 **bosoms:** seios • 8 **stuck out her tongue for shame:** mostrou a língua com vergonha • 9 **aren't they the limit?:** não são o cúmulo? • 10 **discomfited:** desconcertado • 11 **unavoidable breasts:** seios impossíveis de se ignorar • 12 **glared so fiercely that we fled:** nos encarou com tanta fúria que saímos correndo • 13 **to conceal:** ocultar

It wasn't just Certainly-Mary and my parents who had trouble with the English language. My schoolfellows tittered[1] when in my Bombay way I said 'broughtup' for upbringing[2] (as in 'where was your brought-up?') and 'thrice' for three times and 'quarter-plate' for sideplate[3] and 'macaroni' for pasta in general. As for learning the difference between nipples and teats, I really hadn't had any opportunities to increase my word power in that area at all.

5

So I was a little jealous of Certainly-Mary when Mixed-Up came to call. He rang our bell, his body quivering[4] with deference in an old suit grown too loose[5], the trousers tightly gathered[6] by a belt; he had taken off[7] his rubber gloves and there were roses in his hand. My father opened the door and gave him a withering look[8]. Being a snob, Abba was not pleased that the flat lacked[9] a separate service entrance, so that even a porter had to be treated as a member of the same universe as himself.

'Mary,' Mixed-Up managed, licking his lips and pushing back his floppy white hair[10]. 'I, to see Miss Mary, come, am.'

'Wait on,' Abba said, and shut the door in his face.

Certainly-Mary spent all her afternoons off with old Mixed-Up from then on, even though that first date[11] was not a com-

---

1 **tittered:** riam dissimuladamente • 2 **upbringing:** educação • 3 **sideplate:** prato de acompanhamento • 4 **quivering:** tremendo • 5 **too loose:** largo demais • 6 **tightly gathered:** bem ajustada • 7 **he had taken off:** tinha tirado • 8 **gave him a withering look:** o fulminou com o olhar • 9 **lacked:** não tinha • 10 **floppy white hair:** cabelo branco e liso • 11 **first date:** primeiro encontro

plete success. He took her 'up West' to show her the visitors' London she had never seen, but at the top of an up escalator[1] at Piccadilly Circus, while Mecir was painfully enunciating the words on the posters she couldn't read – *Unzip a banana,* and *Idris when I's dri* – she got her sari stuck[2] in the jaws[3] of the machine, and as the escalator pulled at the garment[4] it began to unwind[5]. She was forced to spin round and round like a top[6], and screamed at the top of her voice, 'O BAAP! BAAPU-RÉ! BAAP-RÉ-BAAP-RÉ-BAAP!' It was Mixed-Up who saved her by pushing the emergency stop button before the sari was completely unwound and she was exposed in her petticoat[7] for all the world to see.

'O, courter!' she wept[8] on his shoulder. 'O, no more escaleater, courter, nevermore, surely not!'

My own amorous longings[9] were aimed at Durré's best friend, a Polish girl called Rozalia, who had a holiday job at Faiman's shoe shop on Oxford Street. I pursued her[10] pathetically throughout the holidays and, on and off[11], for the next two years. She would let me have lunch with her sometimes and buy her a Coke and a sandwich, and once she came with me to stand on the terraces[12] at White Hart Lane[13] to watch Jimmy Greaves's[14] first game for the Spurs[15]. 'Come on you whoi-oites,' we both shouted dutifully[16]. 'Come on you *Lily-whoites.*'

---

1 **escalator:** escada rolante • 2 **she got her sari stuck:** ela prendeu o sári • 3 **jaws:** dentes • 4 **garment:** vestimenta • 5 **to unwind:** desenrolar • 6 **she was forced to spin round and round like a top:** foi obrigada a girar e girar como um peão • 7 **petticoat:** anáguas • 8 **she wept:** ela chorou • 9 **longings:** desejos • 10 **I pursued her:** eu a persegui • 11 **on and off:** de forma esporádica • 12 **terraces:** arquibancadas • 13 **White Hart Lane:** estádio de futebol do Tottenham Hotspur • 14 **Jimmy Greaves:** um dos melhores jogadores ingleses de futebol dos anos 1960 • 15 **Spurs:** esporas (apelido do time Tottenham Hotspur) • 16 **dutifully:** como devia ser

After that she even invited me into the back room at Faiman's, where she kissed me twice and let me touch her breast, but that was as far as I got.

And then there was my sort-of-cousin[1] Chandni, whose mother's sister had married my mother's brother, though they had since split up. Chandni was eighteen months older than me, and so sexy it made you sick. She was training to be an Indian classical dancer, Odissi as well as Natyam[2], but in the meantime she dressed in tight black jeans and a clinging black polo-neck jumper[3] and took me, now and then, to hang out[4] at Bunjie's, where she knew most of the folk-music crowd that frequented the place, and where she answered to the name of Moonlight, which is what *chandni* means. I chain-smoked[5] with the folkies[6] and then went to the toilet to throw up[7].

Chandni was the stuff of obsessions. She was a teenage dream, the Moon River come to Earth like the Goddess Ganga, dolled up in slinky black[8]. But for her I was just the young greenhorn[9] cousin to whom she was being nice because he hadn't learned his way around[10].

She-E-rry, won't you come out tonight? yodelled[11] the Four Seasons. I knew exactly how they felt. *Come, come, come out toni-yi-yight.* And while you're at it[12], love me do[13].

---

1 **sort-of-cousin:** espécie de prima • 2 **Odissi, Natyam:** duas das oito danças clássicas da Índia • 3 **clinging black polo-neck jumper:** camisa preta justíssima de gola alta • 4 **to hang out:** sair um tempo (para se divertir) • 5 **I chain-smoked:** fumava sem parar • 6 **folkies:** fãs de música folk • 7 **to throw up:** vomitar • 8 **dolled up in slinky black:** embonecada com uma roupa preta sensual • 9 **greenhorn:** novato • 10 **he hadn't learned his way around:** não sabia se virar ainda • 11 **yodelled:** cantavam no estilo tirolês • 12 **and while you're at it:** e já que você está aí • 13 **love me do:** me ame (também é o título de um dos primeiros sucessos dos *Beatles*)

6

They went for walks in Kensington Gardens. 'Pan[1],' Mixed-Up said, pointing at a statue. 'Los' boy[2]. Nev' grew up[3].' They went to Barkers and Pontings and Derry & Toms and picked out furniture[4] and curtains for imaginary homes. They cruised[5] supermarkets and chose little delicacies[6] to eat. In Mecir's cramped lounge[7] they sipped[8] what he called 'chimpanzee tea' and toasted crumpets[9] in front of an electric bar fire[10].

Thanks to Mixed-Up, Mary was at last able to watch television. She liked children's programmes best, especially *The Flintstones*[11]. Once, giggling at her daring[12], Mary confided to Mixed-Up that Fred and Wilma[13] reminded her of her Sahib[14] and Begum Sahiba[15] upstairs; at which the courter, matching her audaciousness, pointed first at Certainly-Mary and then at himself, grinned a wide gappy smile[16] and said, 'Rubble[17].'

Later, on the news, a vulpine[18] Englishman with a thin moustache and mad eyes declaimed a warning about immigrants, and Certainly-Mary flapped her hand at the set[19]: 'Khali-pili bom marta,' she objected, and then, for her host's

---

1 **Pan:** Peter Pan • 2 **los' boy (lost boy):** garoto perdido • 3 **nev' (never) grew up:** nunca cresceu • 4 **picked out furniture:** escolhiam móveis • 5 **they cruised:** passeavam • 6 **delicacies:** iguarias • 7 **cramped lounge:** sala de visitas pequena • 8 **they sipped:** bebericavam • 9 **crumpets:** tipo de pãozinho inglês comido com manteiga • 10 **electric bar fire:** forno elétrico • 11 *The Flintstones: Os Flintstones* • 12 **giggling at her daring:** rindo de sua própria ousadia • 13 **Fred and Wilma:** Fred e Wilma (Flintstone) • 14 **Sahib:** amo; patrão (híndi) • 15 **Begum Sahiba:** a esposa do patrão (híndi) • 16 **a wide gappy smile:** um largo sorriso desdentado • 17 **Rubble:** sobrenome de Barney e Betty, personagens do desenho • 18 **vulpine:** astuto • 19 **flapped her hand at the set:** agitou a mão para a TV

benefit translated: 'For nothing he is shouting shouting. Bad life! Switch it off.'

They were often interrupted by the Maharajas of B— and P—, who came downstairs to escape their wives and ring other women from the call-box[1] in the porter's room.

'Oh, baby, forget that guy,' said sporty Prince P—, who seemed to spend all his days in tennis whites[2], and whose plump[3] gold Rolex was almost lost in the thick hair on his arm. 'I'll show you a better time than him, baby; step into my world.'

The Maharaja of B— was older, uglier, more matter-of-fact[4]. 'Yes, bring all appliances[5]. Room is booked in name of Mr Douglas Home. Six forty-five to seven fifteen. You have printed rate card[6]? Please. Also a two-foot ruler, must be wooden. Frilly apron[7], plus.'

This is what has lasted in my memory of Waverley House, this seething mass of bad marriages[8], booze[9], philanderers[10] and unfulfilled young lusts[11]; of the Maharaja of P— roaring away towards London's casinoland every night, in a red sports car with fitted blondes[12], and of the Maharaja of B— skulking off[13] to Kensington High Street wearing dark glasses in the dark, and a coat with the collar turned up[14] even though it

---

1 **call-box:** cabine telefônica • 2 **in tennis whites:** com roupa branca de tênis • 3 **plump:** grande; ostensivo • 4 **matter-of-fact:** direto ao ponto • 5 **appliances:** apetrechos • 6 **printed rate card:** cartão com os preços • 7 **frilly apron:** avental com babados • 8 **this seething mass of bad marriages:** essa efervescência de casamentos fracassados • 9 **booze:** bebida alcoólica • 10 **philanderers:** mulherengos • 11 **unfulfilled young lusts:** desejos juvenis insatisfeitos • 12 **red sports car with fitted blondes:** carro esporte vermelho cheio de loiras • 13 **skulking off:** se escondendo por motivos escusos • 14 **with the collar turned up:** com a gola levantada

was high summer; and at the heart of our little universe were Certainly-Mary and her courter, drinking chimpanzee tea and singing along with the national anthem of Bedrock[1].

But they were not really like Barney and Betty Rubble at all. They were formal, polite. They were ... courtly. He courted her, and, like a coy, ringleted ingénue[2] with a fan, she inclined her head, and entertained his suit[3].

7

I spent one half-term[4] weekend in 1963 at the home in Beccles, Suffolk of Field Marshal[5] Sir Charles Lutwidge-Dodgson, an old India hand[6] and a family friend who was supporting my application for British citizenship. 'The Dodo[7]', as he was known, invited me down by myself, saying he wanted to get to know me better.

He was a huge man whose skin had started hanging too loosely on his face, a giant living in a tiny thatched cottage[8] and forever bumping[9] his head. No wonder he was irascible at times; he was in Hell, a Gulliver trapped in that rose-garden Lilliput of croquet hoops[10], church bells, sepia photographs and old battle-trumpets.

The weekend was fitful and awkward[11] until the Dodo asked if I played chess. Slightly awestruck[12] at the prospect of

---

1 **the national anthem of Bedrock:** o hino nacional de Bedrock (cidade dos Flintstones) • 2 **a coy, ringleted ingénue:** jovenzinha arrumada e recatada • 3 **entertained his suit:** aceitava sua corte • 4 **half-term:** metade do período • 5 **Field Marshal:** marechal de campo (cargo militar máximo do Reino Unido) • 6 **an old India hand:** um especialista em Índia • 7 **dodo:** dodó (ave extinta parecida com um peru) • 8 **a tiny thatched cottage:** uma casa de campo minúscula com telhado de sapê • 9 **bumping:** batendo • 10 **croquet hoops:** arcos de *croquet* • 11 **fitful and awkward:** irregular e estranho • 12 **slightly awestruck:** levemente aterrorizado

playing a Field Marshal, I nodded¹; and ninety minutes later, to my amazement, won the game.

I went into the kitchen, strutting somewhat², planning to boast³ a little to the old soldier's long-time housekeeper, Mrs Liddell. But as soon as I entered she said: 'Don't tell me. You never went and won⁴?'

'Yes,' I said, affecting nonchalance⁵. 'As a matter of fact, yes, I did.'

'Gawd,' said Mrs Liddell. 'Now there'll be hell to pay⁶. You go back in there and ask him for another game, and this time make sure you lose.'

I did as I was told, but was never invited to Beccles again.

Still, the defeat of the Dodo gave me new confidence at the chessboard, so when I returned to Waverley House after finishing my O levels⁷, and was at once invited to play a game by Mixed-Up (Mary had told him about my victory in the Battle of Beccles with great pride and some hyperbole), I said: 'Sure, I don't mind.' How long could it take to thrash the old duffer⁸, after all?

There followed a massacre royal⁹. Mixed-Up did not just beat me; he had me for breakfast¹⁰, over easy. I couldn't believe it - the canny opening¹¹, the fluency of his combination play, the force of his attacks, my own impossibly cramped, strangled

---

1 **I nodded:** assenti • 2 **strutting somewhat:** me gabando um pouco • 3 **to boast:** vangloriar-me • 4 **you never went and won?:** você nunca foi e ganhou? • 5 **affecting nonchalance:** fingindo indiferença • 6 **Gawd... now there'll be hell to pay:** Meu Deus... agora vai ser um inferno • 7 **O levels (Ordinary levels):** exames finais (do ensino médio obrigatório no Reino Unido) • 8 **to thrash the old duffer:** para acabar com o velho medíocre • 9 **there followed a massacre royal:** o que se seguiu foi um massacre • 10 **he had me for breakfast:** me engoliu fácil, fácil • 11 **the canny opening:** a saída astuta

positions[1] – and asked for a second game. This time he tucked into me even more heartily[2]. I sat broken in my chair at the end, close to tears. *Big girls don't cry,* I reminded myself, but the song went on playing in my head: *That's just an alibi*[3].

'Who are you?' I demanded, humiliation weighing down every syllable[4]. 'The devil in disguise[5]?'

Mixed-Up gave his big, silly grin. 'Grand Master,' he said. 'Long time. Before head.'

'You're a Grand Master,' I repeated, still in a daze[6]. Then in a moment of horror I remembered that I had seen the name Mecir in books of classic games. 'Nimzo-Indian,' I said aloud. He beamed[7] and nodded furiously.

'That Mecir?' I asked wonderingly[8].

'That,' he said. There was saliva dribbling out of a corner of his sloppy[9] old mouth. This ruined old man was in the books. He was in the books. And even with his mind turned to rubble[10] he could still wipe the floor with me[11].

'Now play lady,' he grinned. I didn't get it[12]. 'Mary lady,' he said. 'Yes yes certainly.'

She was pouring tea, waiting for my answer. 'Aya, you can't play,' I said, bewildered[13].

'Learning, baba,' she said. 'What is it, na? Only a game.'

---

1 **cramped, strangled positions:** posições limitadas, bloqueadas • 2 **he tucked into me even more heartily:** acabou comigo com mais vontade ainda • 3 **alibi:** álibi • 4 **humiliation weighing down every syllable:** a humilhação impregnada em cada sílaba • 5 **the devil in disguise:** o diabo desfarçado • 6 **in a daze:** estupefato • 7 **he beamed:** abriu um grande sorriso • 8 **I asked wonderingly:** perguntei, surpreso • 9 **sloppy:** cheia de baba • 10 **with his mind turned to rubble:** com a mente feita em pedaços • 11 **he could still wipe the floor with me:** ainda podia me fazer de pano de chão • 12 **I didn't get it:** não entendi • 13 **bewildered:** perplexo

And then she, too, beat me senseless[1], and with the black pieces, at that. It was not the greatest day of my life.

8

From *100 Most Instructive Chess Games* by Robert Reshevsky, 1961:

M. Mecir - M. Najdorf
Dallas 1950, Nimzo-Indian Defense

The attack of a tactician can be troublesome[2] to meet – that of a strategist even more so. Whereas the tactician's threats[3] may be unmistakable, the strategist confuses the issue by keeping things in abeyance[4]. He threatens to threaten!

Take this game for instance: Mecir posts a Knight[5] at Q6 to get a grip on[6] the center. Then he establishes a passed Pawn[7] on one wing to occupy his opponent on the Queen side. Finally he stirs up[8] the position on the Kingside. What does the poor bewildered opponent do? How can he defend everything at once? Where will the blow fall[9]?

Watch Mecir keep Najdorf on the run[10], as he shifts[11] the attack from side to side!

Chess had become their private language. Old Mixed-Up, lost as he was for words, retained, on the chessboard, much of the articulacy[12] and subtlety which had vanished from his speech. As Certainly-Mary gained in skill – and she had learned with astonishing speed, I thought bitterly[13], for someone who

---

1 **beat me senseless:** me deu uma surra • 2 **troublesome:** difícil • 3 **threats:** ameaças • 4 **in abeyance:** em suspenso • 5 **Knight:** cavalo (no xadrez) • 6 **to get a grip on:** dominar, controlar • 7 **Pawn:** peão • 8 **he stirs up:** ele muda • 9 **where will the blow fall?:** onde o golpe cairá? • 10 **keep... on the run:** manter sob controle • 11 **he shifts:** ele muda • 12 **articulacy:** eloquência • 13 **I thought bitterly:** pensei amargamente

couldn't read or write or pronounce the letter p - she was better able to understand, and respond to, the wit[1] of the reduced maestro with whom she had so unexpectedly forged a bond[2].

He taught her with great patience, showing-not-telling, repeating openings and combinations and endgame techniques over and over until she began to see the meaning in the patterns. When they played, he handicapped himself[3], he told her her best moves and demonstrated their consequences, drawing her, step by step, into the infinite possibilities of the game.

Such was their courtship[4]. 'It is like an adventure, baba,' Mary once tried to explain to me. 'It is like going with him to his country, you know? What a place, baap-ré! Beautiful and dangerous and funny and full of fuzzles[5]. For me it is a big-big discovery. What to tell you? I go for the game[6]. It is a wonder.'

I understood, then, how far things had gone between them. Certainly-Mary had never married, and had made it clear to old Mixed-Up that it was too late to start any of that monkey business[7] at her age. The courter was a widower, and had grown-up children somewhere, lost long ago behind the ever-higher walls[8] of Eastern Europe. But in the game of chess they had found a form of flirtation, an endless renewal that precluded[9] the possibility of boredom, a courtly wonderland of the ageing heart[10].

What would the Dodo have made of it all[11]? No doubt it

---

1 **wit:** sagacidade • 2 **forged a bond:** forjado um vínculo • 3 **he handicapped himself:** ele baixava seu próprio nível • 4 **courtship:** cortejo • 5 **fuzzles (puzzles):** enigmas • 6 **I go for the game:** eu gosto do jogo • 7 **monkey business:** brincadeiras • 8 **ever-higher walls:** os muros cada vez mais altos • 9 **precluded:** excluía • 10 **a courtly wonderland of the ageing heart:** um paraíso do flerte para um coração maduro • 11 **what would the Dodo have made of it all?:** o que Dodó pensaria de tudo isso

would have scandalised him to see chess, chess of all games, the great formalisation of war, transformed into an art of love.

As for me: my defeats by Certainly-Mary and her courter ushered in further humiliations[1]. Durré and Muneeza went down with the mumps[2], and so, finally, in spite of my mother's efforts to segregate us, did I. I lay terrified in bed while the doctor warned me not to stand up and move around if I could possibly help it[3]. 'If you do,' he said, 'your parents won't need to punish you. You will have punished yourself quite enough.'

I spent the following few weeks tormented day and night by visions of grotesquely swollen[4] testicles and a subsequent life of limp impotence[5] - finished before I'd even started, it wasn't fair[6]! - which were made much worse by my sisters' quick recovery and incessant gibes[7].

But in the end I was lucky; the illness didn't spread to the deep South[8]. 'Think how happy your hundred and one girl-friends will be, bhai[9],' sneered[10] Durré, who knew all about my continued failures in the Rozalia and Chandni departments[11].

On the radio, people were always singing about the joys of being sixteen years old. I wondered where they were, all those boys and girls of my age having the time of their lives. Were they driving around America in Studebaker convertibles[12]? They certainly weren't in my neighbourhood. London, W8 was Sam Cooke[13] country that summer. *Another Saturday*

---

1 **ushered in further humiliations:** prenunciaram mais humilhações • 2 **went down with the mumps:** contraíram caxumba • 3 **if I could possibly help it:** se pudesse evitá-lo de alguma maneira • 4 **swollen:** inchados • 5 **limp impotence:** flácida impotência • 6 **it wasn't fair!:** não era justo! • 7 **incessant gibes:** provocações constantes • 8 **the deep South:** o Sul profundo (os órgãos genitais) • 9 **bhai:** homem (híndi) • 10 **sneered:** desdenhou • 11 **departments:** assuntos • 12 **convertibles:** conversíveis • 13 **Sam Cooke:** cantor de soul

night ... There might be a mop-top love-song¹ stuck at number one, but I was down with lonely Sam in the lower depths of the charts², how-I-wishing I had someone, etc., and generally feeling in a pretty goddamn dreadful way³.

9

'Baba, come quick.'

It was late at night when Aya Mary shook me awake⁴. After many urgent hisses⁵, she managed to drag me out of sleep⁶ and pull me, pajama'ed and yawning⁷, down the hall. On the landing⁸ outside our flat was Mixed-Up the courter, huddled up⁹ against a wall, weeping. He had a black eye¹⁰ and there was dried blood on his mouth.

'What happened?' I asked Mary, shocked.

'Men,' wailed¹¹ Mixed-Up. 'Threaten. Beat.'

He had been in his lounge earlier that evening when the sporting Maharaja of P— burst in¹² to say, 'If anybody comes looking for me, okay, any tough-guy¹³ type guys, okay, I am out, okay? Oh you tea¹⁴. Don't let them go upstairs, okay? Big tip¹⁵, okay?'

A short time later, the old Maharaja of B— also arrived in Mecir's lounge, looking distressed¹⁶.

---

1 **a mop-top love-song:** uma canção de amor no estilo *Beatles* • 2 **the lower depths of the charts:** os últimos lugares na parada de sucessos • 3 **feeling in a pretty goddamn dreadful way:** sentindo-me terrivelmente mal • 4 **shook me awake:** me despertou com sacudidas • 5 **urgent hisses:** sussurros insistentes • 6 **she managed to drag me out of sleep:** conseguiu me tirar do sono • 7 **pajama'ed and yawning:** de pijama e bocejando • 8 **landing:** terreno • 9 **huddled up:** agachado • 10 **a black eye:** um olho roxo • 11 **wailed:** gemeu • 12 **burst in:** irrompeu • 13 **tough-guy:** durão • 14 **oh you tea (O-U-T):** fora • 15 **big tip:** boa gorjeta • 16 **distressed:** angustiado

'Suno, listen on,' said the Maharaja of B—. 'You don't know where I am, samajh liya[1]? Understood? Some low persons may inquire[2]. You don't know. I am abroad, achha[3]? On extended travels abroad. Do your job, porter. Handsome recompense[4].'

Late at night two tough-guy types did indeed turn up[5]. It seemed the hairy Prince P— had gambling debts[6]. 'Out,' Mixed-Up grinned in his sweetest way. The tough-guy types nodded, slowly. They had long hair and thick lips like Mick Jagger's. 'He's a busy gent[7]. We should of made an appointment,' said the first type to the second. 'Didn't I tell you we should of called?'

'You did,' agreed the second type. 'Got to do these things right, you said, he's royalty. And you was right, my son, I put my hand up[8], I was dead wrong[9]. I put my hand up to that.'

'Let's leave our card,' said the first type. 'Then he'll know to expect us.'

'Ideal,' said the second type, and smashed his fist[10] into old Mixed-Up's mouth. 'You tell him,' the second type said, and struck the old man in the eye. 'When he's in[11]. You mention it.'

He had locked the front door after that; but much later, well after midnight, there was a hammering[12].

Mixed-Up called out, 'Who?'

'We are close friends of the Maharaja of B—' said a voice. 'No, I tell a lie. Acquaintances[13].'

---

1 **samajh liya?:** entendido? (híndi) • 2 **some low persons may inquire:** gente má pode perguntar por mim • 3 **achha?:** certo (híndi) • 4 **handsome recompense:** recompensa generosa • 5 **did indeed turn up:** de fato apareceram • 6 **gambling debts:** dívidas de jogo • 7 **a busy gent:** um cavalheiro muito ocupado • 8 **I put my hand up:** dou o braço a torcer • 9 **I was dead wrong:** eu estava totalmente equivocado • 10 **smashed his fist:** deu um soco • 11 **when he's in:** quando ele estiver aí • 12 **a hammering:** batidas fortes na porta • 13 **acquaintances:** conhecidos

'He calls upon a lady of our acquaintance[1],' said a second voice. 'To be precise.'

'It is in that connection that we crave audience[2],' said the first voice.

'Gone,' said Mecir. 'Jet plane. Gone.'

There was a silence. Then the second voice said, 'Can't be in the jet set if you never jump on a jet, eh? Biarritz, Monte, all of that.'

'Be sure and let His Highness know', said the first voice, 'that we eagerly[3] await his return.'

'With regard to our mutual friend,' said the second voice. 'Eagerly.'

What does the poor bewildered opponent do? The words from the chess book popped unbidden into my head[4]. *How can he defend everything at once? Where will the blow fall? Watch Mecir keep Najdorf on the run, as he shifts the attack from side to side!*

Mixed-Up returned to his lounge and on this occasion, even though there had been no use of force, he began to weep. After a time he took the elevator up to the fourth floor and whispered through our letterbox[5] to Certainly-Mary sleeping on her mat.

'I didn't want to wake Sahib,' Mary said. 'You know his trouble, na? And Begum Sahiba is so tired at end of the day. So now you tell, baba, what to do?'

What did she expect me to come up with[6]? I was sixteen

---

1 **he calls upon a lady of our acquaintance:** costuma visitar uma dama que conhecemos • 2 **we crave audience:** solicitamos audiência • 3 **eagerly:** impacientemente • 4 **popped unbidden into my head:** surgiram na minha cabeça sem serem convidadas • 5 **letterbox:** caixa de correio • 6 **what did she expect me to come up with?:** que ideia brilhante ele achava que eu ia ter?

years old. 'Mixed-Up must call the police,' I unoriginally offered.

'No, no, baba,' said Certainly-Mary emphatically. 'If the courter makes a scandal for Maharaja-log, then in the end it is the courter only who will be out on his ear[1].'

I had no other ideas. I stood before them feeling like a fool, while they both turned upon me their frightened, supplicant eyes.

'Go to sleep,' I said. 'We'll think about it in the morning.' *The first pair of thugs[2] were tacticians,* I was thinking. *They were troublesome to meet. But the second pair were scarier; they were strategists. They threatened to threaten.*

Nothing happened in the morning, and the sky was clear. It was almost impossible to believe in fists[3], and menacing voices at the door. During the course of the day both Maharajas visited the porter's lounge and stuck five-pound notes[4] in Mixed-Up's waistcoat[5] pocket.

'Held the fort[6], good man,' said Prince P—, and the Maharaja of B— echoed those sentiments: 'Spot on[7]. All handled now, achha[8]? Problem over.'

The three of us - Aya Mary, her courter, and me - held a council of war[9] that afternoon and decided that no further action was necessary. The hall porter was the front line in any such situation, I argued, and the front line had held[10]. And

---

1 **will be out on his ear:** que vai acabar sendo jogado na rua • 2 **thugs:** bandidos • 3 **fists:** punhos • 4 **stuck five-pound notes:** colocaram notas de cinco libras • 5 **waistcoat:** jaleco • 6 **held the fort:** defendeu o forte • 7 **spot on:** isso mesmo • 8 **all handled now, achha?:** tudo resolvido agora, certo? • 9 **held a council of war:** nos reunimos em um conselho de guerra • 10 **the front line had held:** a primeira linha havia resistido

now the risks were past. Assurances had been given. End of story.

'End of story,' repeated Certainly-Mary doubtfully, but then, seeking to reassure Mecir, she brightened[1]. 'Correct,' she said. 'Most certainly! All-done, finis.' She slapped her hands against each other for emphasis. She asked Mixed-Up if he wanted a game of chess; but for once the courter didn't want to play.

10

After that I was distracted, for a time, from the story of Mixed-Up and Certainly-Mary by violence nearer home.

My middle sister Muneeza, now eleven, was entering her delinquent phase a little early. She was the true inheritor of my father's black rage[2], and when she lost control it was terrible to behold[3]. That summer she seemed to pick fights[4] with my father on purpose; seemed prepared, at her young age, to test her strength against his. (I intervened in her rows[5] with Abba only once, in the kitchen. She grabbed the kitchen scissors and flung them at me[6]. They cut me on the thigh[7]. After that I kept my distance.)

As I witnessed their wars I felt myself coming unstuck from[8] the idea of family itself. I looked at my screaming sister and thought how brilliantly self-destructive she was, how triumphantly she was ruining her relations with the people she needed most.

---

1 **she brightened:** se animou • 2 **black rage:** fúria cega • 3 **to behold:** observar • 4 **to pick fights:** buscar brigas • 5 **rows:** discussões • 6 **she grabbed the kitchen scissors and flung them at me:** ela pegou as tesouras da cozinha e jogou-as em cima de mim • 7 **thigh:** coxa • 8 **I felt myself coming unstuck from:** sentia que me desapegava de

And I looked at my choleric, face-pulling[1] father and thought about British citizenship. My existing Indian passport permitted me to travel only to a very few countries, which were carefully listed on the second right-hand page. But I might soon have a British passport and then, by hook or by crook[2], I would get away from him. I would not have this face-pulling in my life.

At sixteen, you still think you can escape from your father. You aren't listening to his voice speaking through your mouth, you don't see how your gestures already mirror[3] his; you don't see him in the way you hold your body, in the way you sign your name. You don't hear his whisper in your blood.

On the day I have to tell you about, my two-year-old sister Chhoti Scheherazade, Little Scare-zade, started crying as she often did during one of our family rows. Amma and Aya Mary loaded her into her push-chair[4] and made a rapid get-away[5]. They pushed her to Kensington Square and then sat on the grass, turned Scheherazade loose[6] and made philosophical remarks[7] while she tired herself out. Finally, she fell asleep, and they made their way home[8] in the fading light[9] of the evening. Outside Waverley House they were approached by two well-turned-out[10] young men with Beatle haircuts and the buttoned-up, collarless jackets[11] made popular by the band. The first of these young men asked my mother, very politely, if she might be the Maharani of B——.

---

1 **face-pulling:** fazendo caretas • 2 **by hook or by crook:** por bem ou por mal • 3 **mirror:** imitam • 4 **push-chair:** carrinho de bebê • 5 **made a rapid get-away:** saíram correndo • 6 **turned... loose:** soltaram • 7 **remarks:** comentários • 8 **made their way home:** voltaram para casa • 9 **fading light:** no lusco-fusco • 10 **well-turned-out:** bem-vestidos • 11 **collarless jackets:** jaquetas sem gola (estilo Mao)

'No,' my mother answered, flattered[1].

'Oh, but you are, madam,' said the second Beatle, equally politely. 'For you are heading for[2] Waverley House and that is the Maharaja's place of residence.'

'No, no,' my mother said, still blushing with pleasure. 'We are a different Indian family.'

'Quite so[3],' the first Beatle nodded understandingly, and then, to my mother's great surprise, placed a finger alongside his nose, and winked[4]. 'Incognito, eh. Mum's the word[5].'

'Now excuse us,' my mother said, losing patience. 'We are not the ladies you seek.'

The second Beatle tapped a foot[6] lightly against a wheel of the push-chair. 'Your husband seeks ladies, madam, were you aware of that fact? Yes, he does. Most assiduously, may I add.'

'Too assiduously,' said the first Beatle, his face darkening.

'I tell you I am not the Maharani Begum,' my mother said, growing suddenly alarmed. 'Her business is not my business. Kindly let me pass[7].'

The second Beatle stepped closer to her. She could feel his breath, which was minty[8]. 'One of the ladies he sought out[9] was our ward[10], as you might say,' he explained. 'That would be the term. Under our protection, you follow. Us, therefore, being responsible for her welfare[11].'

'Your husband', said the first Beatle, showing his teeth in a frightening way, and raising his voice one notch[12], 'damaged

---

1 **flattered:** lisonjeada • 2 **heading for:** indo na direção de • 3 **quite so:** percebe-se • 4 **winked:** piscou um olho • 5 **mum's the word:** boca de siri • 6 **tapped a foot:** bateu o pé levemente • 7 **kindly let me pass:** faça o favor de me deixar passar • 8 **minty:** mentolado • 9 **he sought out:** ele foi atrás de • 10 **ward:** pupila • 11 **welfare:** bem-estar • 12 **raising his voice one notch:** elevando um pouco o tom de voz

the goods[1]. Do you hear me, Queenie[2]? He damaged the fucking goods.'

'Mistaken identity, fleas,' said Certainly-Mary. 'Many Indian residents in Waverley House. We are decent ladies; *fleas*.'

The second Beatle had taken out something from an inside pocket. A blade caught the light[3]. 'Fucking wogs[4],' he said. 'You fucking come over here, you don't fucking know how to fucking behave. Why don't you fucking fuck off to fucking Wogistan? Fuck your fucking wog arses[5]. Now then,' he added in a quiet voice, holding up the knife[6], 'unbutton your blouses[7].'

Just then a loud noise emanated from the doorway of Waverley House. The two women and the two men turned to look, and out came Mixed-Up, yelling at the top of his voice and windmilling his arms[8] like a mad old loon[9].

'Hullo,' said the Beatle with the knife, looking amused. 'Who's this, then? Oh oh fucking seven[10]?'

Mixed-Up was trying to speak, he was in a mighty agony of effort, but all that was coming out of his mouth was raw, unshaped noise[11]. Scheherazade woke up and joined in. The two Beatles looked displeased. But then something happened inside old Mixed-Up; something popped[12], and in a great rush he gabbled[13], 'Sirs sirs no sirs these not B— women sirs B—

---

1 **damaged the goods:** estragou a mercadoria • 2 **Queenie:** rainha • 3 **a blade caught the light:** a luz refletiu em uma lâmina • 4 **fucking wogs:** expressão racista para denominar pessoas de pele escura • 5 **arses:** traseiros • 6 **holding up the knife:** ameaçando com a faca • 7 **unbutton your blouses:** desabotoem as blusas • 8 **windmilling his arms:** agitando os braços • 9 **loon:** lunático • 10 **oh oh fucking seven?:** 007 de merda? • 11 **raw, unshaped noise:** ruído primitivo e indefinido • 12 **something popped:** alguma coisa fez *clic* • 13 **in a great rush he gabbled:** de repente ele desatou a falar

women upstairs on floor three sirs Maharaja of B— also sirs God's truth mother's grave swear.'

It was the longest sentence he had spoken since the stroke[1] that had broken his tongue long ago.

And what with his torrent and Scheherazade's squalls[2] there were suddenly heads poking out[3] from doorways, attention was being paid, and the two Beatles nodded gravely[4]. 'Honest mistake,' the first of them said apologetically to my mother, and actually bowed from the waist[5]. 'Could happen to anyone,' the knife-man added, ruefully[6]. They turned and began to walk quickly away. As they passed Mecir, however; they paused. 'I know you, though,' said the knife-man. ' *"Jet plane. Gone."* ' He made a short movement of the arm, and then Mixed-Up the courter was lying on the pavement[7] with blood leaking from a wound[8] in his stomach. 'All okay now,' he gasped, and passed out[9].

II

He was on the road to recovery by Christmas; my mother's letter to the landlords[10], in which she called him a 'knight in shining armour[11]', ensured that he was well looked after, and his job was kept open for him. He continued to live in his little ground-floor cubby-hole[12], while the hall porter's duties were carried out by shift-duty staff[13]. 'Nothing but the best

---

1 **stroke:** derrame cerebral • 2 **squalls:** gritos • 3 **poking out:** saindo; aparecendo • 4 **nodded gravely:** assentiram com seriedade • 5 **bowed from the waist:** fez uma reverência • 6 **ruefully:** sombriamente • 7 **pavement:** calçada • 8 **with blood leaking from a wound:** com sangue escorrendo de uma ferida • 9 **passed out:** desmaiou • 10 **landlords:** proprietários • 11 **a knight in shining armour:** um cavaleiro com armadura reluzente • 12 **cubby-hole:** cubículo • 13 **shift-duty staff:** por uma equipe que trabalhava em turnos

for our very own hero,' the landlords assured my mother in their reply.

The two Maharajas and their retinues had moved out[1] before I came home for the Christmas holidays, so we had no further visits from the Beatles or the Rolling Stones. Certainly-Mary spent as much time as she could with Mecir; but it was the look of my old Aya that worried me more than poor Mixed-Up. She looked older, and powdery[2], as if she might crumble away[3] at any moment into dust.

'We didn't want to worry you at school,' my mother said. 'She has been having heart trouble. Palpitations. Not all the time, but.'

Mary's health problems had sobered up[4] the whole family. Muneeza's tantrums[5] had stopped, and even my father was making an effort. They had put up a Christmas tree in the sitting-room and decorated it with all sorts of baubles[6]. It was so odd[7] to see a Christmas tree at our place that I realised things must be fairly serious.

On Christmas Eve my mother suggested that Mary might like it if we all sang some carols[8]. Amma had made songsheets, six copies, by hand. When we did *O come, all ye faithful* I showed off[9] by singing from memory in Latin. Everybody behaved perfectly. When Muneeza suggested that we should try *Swinging on a Star* or *I Wanna Hold Your Hand* instead of this boring stuff, she wasn't really being serious. So this is family life, I thought. This is it.

But we were only play-acting[10].

---

1 **their retinues had moved out:** seus séquitos tinham se mudado • 2 **powdery:** quebradiço • 3 **crumble away:** desfazer-se • 4 **had sobered up:** tinham endireitado • 5 **tantrums:** explosões de humor • 6 **baubles:** adornos • 7 **odd:** estranho • 8 **carols:** canções de Natal • 9 **I showed off:** eu me exibi • 10 **play-acting:** fingindo

A few weeks earlier, at school, I'd come across¹ an American boy, the star of the school's Rugby football team, crying in the Chapel cloisters². I asked him what the matter was and he told me that President Kennedy had been assassinated. 'I don't believe you,' I said, but I could see that it was true. The football star sobbed³ and sobbed. I took his hand.

'When the President dies, the nation is orphaned,' he eventually said, broken-heartedly parroting a piece of cracker-barrel wisdom⁴ he'd probably heard on Voice of America⁵.

'I know how you feel,' I lied. 'My father just died, too.'

Mary's heart trouble turned out to be a mystery; unpredictably, it came and went. She was subjected to all sorts of tests during the next six months, but each time the doctors ended up by shaking their heads⁶: they couldn't find anything wrong with her. Physically, she was right as rain⁷; except that there were these periods when her heart kicked and bucked in her chest⁸ like the wild horses in *The Misfits*⁹, the ones whose roping and tying¹⁰ made Marilyn Monroe so mad.

Mecir went back to work in the spring, but his experience had knocked the stuffing out of him¹¹. He was slower to smile, duller of eye¹², more inward¹³. Mary, too, had turned in upon herself¹⁴. They still met for tea, crumpets and *The Flintstones,* but something was no longer quite right.

---

1 **I'd come across:** encontrei • 2 **cloisters:** claustros • 3 **sobbed:** soluçava • 4 **parroting a piece of cracker-barrel wisdom:** repetindo como um papagaio um clichê de sabedoria de botequim • 5 **Voice of America:** emissora oficial do governo norte-americano • 6 **shaking their heads:** negando com a cabeça • 7 **she was right as rain:** estava tudo em ordem • 8 **her heart kicked and bucked in her chest:** o coração pulava e chutava em seu peito • 9 ***The Misfits:*** *Os desajustados* (filme de 1961) • 10 **roping and tying:** caçados a laço e amarrados • 11 **had knocked the stuffing out of him:** o havia deixado sem brilho algum • 12 **duller of eye:** mais lento nas reações • 13 **more inward:** mais introvertido • 14 **had turned in upon herself:** tinha se tornado reservada

At the beginning of the summer Mary made an announcement.

'I know what is wrong with me,' she told my parents, out of the blue[1]. 'I need to go home.'

'But, Aya,' my mother argued, 'homesickness[2] is not a real disease.'

'God knows for what-all we came over to this country,' Mary said. 'But I can no longer stay. No. Certainly not.' Her determination was absolute.

So it was England that was breaking her heart, breaking it by not being India. London was killing her, by not being Bombay. And Mixed-Up? I wondered. Was the courter killing her, too, because he was no longer himself? Or was it that her heart, roped[3] by two different loves, was being pulled both East and West, whinnying and rearing[4], like those movie horses being yanked[5] this way by Clark Gable and that way by Montgomery Clift, and she knew that to live she would have to choose?

'I must go,' said Certainly-Mary. 'Yes, certainly. *Bas*[6]. Enough.'

That summer, the summer of '64, I turned seventeen. Chandni went back to India. Durré's Polish friend Rozalia informed me over a sandwich[7] in Oxford Street that she was getting engaged to a 'real man', so I could forget about seeing her again, because this Zbigniew was the jealous type. Roy Orbison sang *It's Over* in my ears as I walked away to the Tube[8], but the truth was that nothing had really begun.

---

1 **out of the blue:** do nada • 2 **homesickness:** saudades de casa • 3 **roped:** amarrado • 4 **whinnying and rearing:** relinchando e dando coices • 5 **being yanked:** sendo puxado • 6 *bas*: basta (híndi) • 7 **over a sandwich:** enquanto comiam um sanduíche • 8 **the Tube:** o metrô de Londres

Certainly-Mary left us in mid-July. My father bought her a one-way ticket to Bombay, and that last morning was heavy with the pain of ending. When we took her bags down to the car, Mecir the hall porter was nowhere to be seen. Mary did not knock on the door of his lounge, but walked straight out through the freshly polished oak-panelled lobby[1], whose mirrors and brasses[2] were sparkling brightly; she climbed into the back seat of our Ford Zodiac and sat there stiffly[3] with her carry-on grip on her lap[4], staring straight ahead. I had known and loved her all my life. *Never mind your damned courter[5]*, I wanted to shout at her, *what about me?*

As it happened, she was right about the homesickness. After her return to Bombay, she never had a day's heart trouble again; and, as the letter from her niece Stella confirmed, at ninety-one she was still going strong[6].

Soon after she left, my father told us he had decided to 'shift location' to Pakistan. As usual, there were no discussions, no explanations, just the simple fiat[7]. He gave up the lease[8] on the flat in Waverley House at the end of the summer holidays, and they all went off to Karachi, while I went back to school.

I became a British citizen that year. I was one of the lucky ones, I guess, because in spite of that chess game I had the Dodo on my side. And the passport did, in many ways, set me free. It allowed me to come and go, to make choices that

---

1 **freshly polished oak-panelled lobby:** painéis de carvalho recém-encerados da entrada • 2 **mirrors and brasses:** espelhos e metais • 3 **stiffly:** erguida • 4 **with her carry-on grip on her lap:** com a bolsa no colo • 5 **never mind your damned courter:** não me importa seu maldito porteiro (courter) • 6 **she was still going strong:** ainda estava em plena forma • 7 **fiat:** decisão imposta (termo militar) • 8 **he gave up the lease:** largou o aluguel

were not the ones my father would have wished. But I, too, have ropes around my neck[1], I have them to this day, pulling me this way and that, East and West, the nooses tightening[2], commanding[3], *choose, choose.*

I buck, I snort, I whinny, I rear, I kick[4]. Ropes, I do not choose between you. Lassoes, lariats[5], I choose neither of you, and both. Do you hear? I refuse to choose.

A year or so after we moved out I was in the area and dropped in at Waverley House to see how the old courter was doing. Maybe, I thought, we could have a game of chess, and he could beat me to a pulp[6]. The lobby was empty, so I knocked on the door of his little lounge. A stranger answered.

'Where's Mixed-Up?' I cried, taken by surprise. I apologised at once, embarrassed. 'Mr Mecir, I meant, the porter.'

'I'm the porter, sir,' the man said. 'I don't know anything about any mix-up.'

---

1 **I, too, have ropes around my neck:** eu também tenho cordas no pescoço • 2 **the nooses tightening:** os nós se apertando • 3 **commanding:** ordenando • 4 **I buck, I snort, I whinny, I rear, I kick:** eu pulo, eu esbaforejo, eu relincho, eu empino, eu dou coices • 5 **lassoes, lariats:** laços para amarrar cavalos • 6 **he could beat me to a pulp:** podia fazer picadinho de mim

Philip Roth
Defender of the Faith

"With a kind of quiet nervousness, they polished shoes, shined belt buckles, squared away underwear, trying as best they could to accept their fate."

Philip Milton Roth (Newark, Nova Jersey, 1933) teve uma infância asfixiante mas segura na sua cidade natal, epicentro de todas as suas histórias. Asfixiante porque, como diria Sheldon Grossbart, protagonista de "Defender of the Faith", asfixiar os filhos debaixo do terrível manto da superproteção é tudo o que fazem os pais judeus. Assim, Roth teve uma infância protegida e uma adolescência sem sobressaltos dedicada ao estudo da literatura inglesa (primeiro na Universidade de Bucknell e, em seguida, na de Chicago). Após obter seu doutorado, dedicou-se a ensinar escrita criativa na Universidade de Iowa e em Princeton, e literatura comparada na Pensilvânia. Aposentou-se em 1991, seis anos antes de ganhar o Prêmio Pulitzer por *Pastoral americana*, seu clássico mais reconhecido pela crítica.

Mas muito antes disso, serviu na Marinha norte-americana durante dois anos e escreveu relatos e críticas de cinema para revistas como *The New Republic*. Suas experiências na Marinha se converteram no seu primeiro romance, *Adeus, Colombus*, editado em 1959 e composto, na verdade, por uma novela e cinco contos, entre os quais se destaca "Defender of the Faith". O romance mereceu críticas fabulosas, de que Roth só começaria a desfrutar com a publicação do seu quarto livro, o romance *O complexo de portnoy*, em 1969. Naquela época já havia conhecido Saul Bellow em Chicago e Margaret Martinson, com quem se casou em 1960 e, em pouco tempo (1963), de quem se divorciou. Sua morte trágica, em 1968, num acidente de trânsito, marcou a literatura de Roth. Muitos dos seus personagens femininos dessa época são baseados nela (Lucy Nelson de *When She Was Good* [*Quando ela era boa*], seu terceiro romance, por exemplo, e Maureen Tarnopol de *My Life As a Man* [*Minha vida como homem*] de 1974).

Durante a década de 1970, experimentou tudo o que pôde. Nesses anos escreveu desde sátira política *Our Gang* [*Nossa turma*, 1971] até pequenos desvios kafkianos como *The Breast* [*O peito*, 1972], a história de um homem que acorda numa manhã transformado num gigantesco peito de mulher. Na mesma década criou aquele que acabaria se tornando o *alter ego* do autor: Nathan Zuckerman. Zuckerman protagonizará (ou aparecerá como personagem secundário) em toda a produção de Roth entre 1979 e 1986. *The Ghost Writer* (que teve uma edição brasileira, já esgotada, sob o título *Diário de uma ilusão*), *Pastoral americana* e *Casei com um comunista* são suas peripécias mais famosas. Escritos já nos anos 1990 (o primeiro recebeu um celebrado Pulitzer; o segundo é uma história de vingança pessoal) compõem, junto com *O avesso da vida*, de 1986, *A marca humana* e *Fantasma sai de cena*, 2007, uma pentalogia particular Zuckerman.

Em 1990 casou-se com a atriz britânica Claire Bloom, de quem se separou quatro anos depois. A moça não tardou em converter até o último detalhe do seu casamento com Roth (na época já um eterno candidato ao Nobel) no livro chamado *Leaving a Doll's House*, que fez a alegria da imprensa sensacionalista. O escritor deu sua particular e magistral versão do assunto em *Casei com um comunista*. Nos últimos anos, Roth soltou as rédeas da sua incansável pena, assinando praticamente um livro por ano, entre eles *Homem comum* e o mais recente *A Humilhação*, de 2009.

LAURA FERNÁNDEZ

APRESENTAÇÃO DO CONTO
Defender of the Faith

Sheldon Grossbart é um bom menino. Ou ao menos parece ser. A única coisa que quer é seguir levando sua vida como o faria se estivesse em casa. Com a particularidade de ser judeu. E tem algo mais: ele está prestes a ser enviado para o *front*. Duas semanas depois de terminar a Segunda Guerra Mundial, o sargento Nathan Marx, também judeu, é enviado ao acampamento militar de Crowder, no estado do Missouri. Ali conhece Sheldon Grossbart, soldado raso, dezenove anos recém-completados, e desde o primeiro momento se sente à mercê do jovem. Sheldon utiliza sua condição de judeu para encurralar o Sargento Marx e o resto do pelotão.

Primeiro quer se livrar de limpar os barracões às sextas-feiras à tarde porque é o dia de ir à sinagoga ouvir o rabino. "Você sabe como é, senhor", alfineta. "Não me chame de senhor, me chame de sargento", responde Marx, pensando no seu íntimo: "O rapaz tem razão, sou um deles." Após conseguir se livrar dos barracões e assistir sem prestar atenção ao culto na sinagoga, Sheldon vai um pouco além e pede comida diferente. "Nós, judeus, não podemos comer isso", comenta, "você já ouviu o rabino". A fase seguinte será escrever à Casa Branca assinando como seu pai, que não sabia uma palavra de inglês. "Já sabe como são as famílias judias", se desculpa após Marx chamar sua atenção.

Aonde Sheldon quer chegar? Que diabos quer do Sargento Marx? "Defender of the Faith", um dos contos mais aclamados de Philip Roth, captura a luta interna daquele que se rebela contra a sua própria condição (neste caso, o judaísmo) sem deixar de se sentir ligado sentimentalmente a ela. Porque Nathan Marx funciona à perfeição como *alter ego* do próprio Roth, empenhado em tentar viver como os demais, porém incapaz de abandonar aquilo sem o que não seria o que é. Publicado pela primeira vez em 1960 na *The New Yorker*, a revista que alçou à moda o conto nas décadas de 1950 e 60, e posteriormente incluído em *Adeus, Columbus*, "Defender of the Faith" não é apenas a história de um *rat racer*, um jovenzinho sem escrúpulos capaz de converter as pessoas em bonecos com quem brinca quando quer, mas é também a fotografia torta de um momento, o canto da sala que não foi varrido de um episódio histórico (a Segunda Guerra Mundial) que esteve a ponto de deixar o mundo em pedaços. Por acaso, pode um judeu utilizar o Holocausto para livrar-se de lutar a favor daqueles que querem libertar seu povo? Sim: ele se chama Sheldon Grossbart, e gosta de jantar num restaurante chinês.

Emocionante e brutal, "Defender of the Faith" se constrói a partir das conversas mantidas entre o sargento Marx e o soldado Grossbart e de algumas cenas na sala do sargento, nos refeitórios do acampamento e, claro, na sinagoga. O vocabulário que Roth utiliza é simples, e você pode se valer do glossário incluído em cada página desta edição para se aprofundar em referências culturais ídiches e esclarecer possíveis dúvidas. Vale mencionar a formidável carta que Sheldon envia à Casa Branca, fingindo ser seu pai aflito, da qual sem dúvida você vai desfrutar sem conseguir evitar o riso quando escutar a versão em áudio do conto. Pronto para saber que fim leva o rapaz esperto? Uma pista: às vezes o mundo é (in)justo demais.

LAURA FERNÁNDEZ

Defender of the Faith

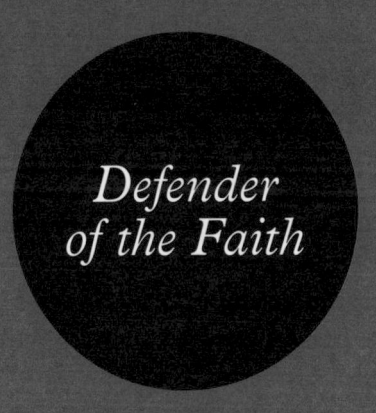

I

IN MAY OF 1945, ONLY A FEW WEEKS AFTER the fighting had ended in Europe, I was rotated back[1] to the States, where I spent the remainder of the war with a training company at Camp Crowder, Missouri. Along with the rest of the Ninth Army, I had been racing across Germany so swiftly[2] during the late winter and spring that when I boarded the plane, I couldn't believe its destination lay to the west. My mind might inform me otherwise, but there was an inertia of the spirit that told me we were flying to a new front, where we would disembark and continue our push eastward[3] — eastward until we'd circled the globe, marching through villages along whose twisting, cobbled streets[4] crowds of the enemy would watch us take possession of what, up till then, they'd considered their own. I had changed enough in two years not to mind[5] the trembling of old people, the crying of the very young, the uncertainty and fear in the eyes of the once arrogant. I had been fortunate enough to develop an infantryman's heart[6], which, like his feet, at first aches and swells[7] but finally grows horny enough[8] for him to travel the weirdest paths[9] without feeling a thing.

---

1 **I was rotated back:** fui levado de volta • 2 **swiftly:** rapidamente • 3 **eastward:** em direção ao leste • 4 **twisting, cobbled streets:** ruas tortuosas de paralelepípedo • 5 **to mind:** ser afetado • 6 **an infantryman's heart:** um coração de soldado • 7 **aches and swells:** dói e incha • 8 **grows horny enough:** se endurece o suficiente • 9 **the weirdest paths:** os caminhos mais estranhos

Captain Paul Barrett was my C.O.[1] in Camp Crowder. The day I reported for duty, he came out of his office to shake my hand. He was short, gruff[2], and fiery[3], and — indoors or out — he wore his polished helmet liner[4] pulled down to his little eyes. In Europe, he had received a battlefield commission[5] and a serious chest wound[6], and he'd been returned to the States only a few months before. He spoke easily to me, and at the evening formation he introduced me to the troops. "Gentlemen," he said. "Sergeant Thurston, as you know, is no longer with this company. Your new first sergeant is Sergeant Nathan Marx, here. He is a veteran of the European theater, and consequently will expect to find a company of soldiers here, and not a company of *boys*."

I sat up late in the orderly room[7] that evening, trying halfheartedly[8] to solve the riddle of duty rosters[9], personnel forms, and morning reports. The Charge of Quarters[10] slept with his mouth open on a mattress on the floor. A trainee stood reading the next day's duty roster, which was posted on the bulletin board[11] just inside the screen door[12]. It was a warm evening, and I could hear radios playing dance music over in the barracks[13]. The trainee, who had been staring at me whenever he thought I wouldn't notice, finally took a step in my direction.

---

1 **C.O. (Commanding Officer):** oficial de comando • 2 **gruff:** rude • 3 **fiery:** apaixonado • 4 **polished helmet liner:** capacete interior lustrado • 5 **a battlefield commission:** uma condecoração • 6 **a serious chest wound:** um ferimento grave no peito • 7 **I sat up late in the orderly room:** fiquei até tarde na sala de comando • 8 **halfheartedly:** com pouca motivação • 9 **the riddle of duty rosters:** o quebra-cabeças dos turnos de trabalho • 10 **The Charge of Quarters:** o responsável administrativo do quartel • 11 **bulletin board:** quadro de avisos • 12 **screen door:** porta de tela • 13 **barracks:** quartel

"Hey, Sarge — we having a G.I. party[1] tomorrow night?" he asked. A G.I. party is a barracks cleaning.

"You usually have them on Friday nights?" I asked him.

"Yes," he said, and then he added, mysteriously, "that's the whole thing."

"Then you'll have a G.I. party."

He turned away, and I heard him mumbling[2]. His shoulders were moving and I wondered if he was crying.

"What's your name, soldier?" I asked.

He turned, not crying at all. Instead, his green-speckled eyes[3], long and narrow, flashed like fish in the sun. He walked over to me and sat on the edge of my desk. He reached out a hand[4]. "Sheldon," he said.

"Stand on your feet, Sheldon."

Getting off the desk[5], he said, "Sheldon Grossbart." He smiled at the familiarity into which he'd led me.

"You against cleaning the barracks Friday night, Grossbart?" I said. "Maybe we shouldn't have G.I. parties. Maybe we should get a maid[6]." My tone startled me[7]. I felt I sounded like every top sergeant I had ever known.

"No, Sergeant." He grew serious, but with a seriousness that seemed to be only the stifling of a smile[8]. "It's just — G.I. parties on Friday night, of all nights."

He slipped up onto the corner[9] of the desk again — not quite sitting, but not quite standing, either. He looked at me with those speckled eyes flashing, and then made a gesture

---

1 **G.I. (Government Issue) party:** festa de soldados • 2 **mumbling:** murmurando • 3 **green-speckled eyes:** olhos verde-claros • 4 **he reached out a hand:** estendeu a mão • 5 **getting off the desk:** levantando-se da mesa • 6 **maid:** empregada • 7 **startled me:** me surpreendeu • 8 **the stifling of a smile:** um sorriso contido • 9 **he slipped up onto the corner:** se apoiou na quina

with his hands. It was very slight — no more than a movement back and forth of the wrist — and yet it managed to exclude from our affairs everything else in the orderly room, to make the two of us the center of the world. It seemed, in fact, to exclude everything even about the two of us except our hearts.

"Sergeant Thurston was one thing," he whispered, glancing[1] at the sleeping C.Q.[2], "but we thought that with you here things might be a little different."

"We?"

"The Jewish personnel."

"Why?" I asked, harshly[3]. "What's on your mind?" Whether I was still angry at the "Sheldon" business, or now at something else, I hadn't time to tell, but clearly I was angry.

"We thought you — Marx, you know, like Karl Marx. The Marx Brothers. Those guys are all — M-a-r-x. Isn't that how *you* spell it, Sergeant?"

"M-a-r-x."

"Fishbein said —" He stopped. "What I mean to say, Sergeant —" His face and neck were red, and his mouth moved but no words came out. In a moment, he raised himself to attention[4], gazing down at me[5]. It was as though he had suddenly decided he could expect no more sympathy from me than from Thurston, the reason being that I was of Thurston's faith, and not his. The young man had managed to confuse himself as to what my faith really was, but I felt no desire to straighten him out[6]. Very simply, I didn't like him.

---

1 **glancing:** lançando um olhar • 2 **C.Q. (Charge of Quarters):** o responsável administrativo do quartel • 3 **harshly:** severamente • 4 **he raised himself to attention:** ele ficou em estado de atenção • 5 **gazing down at me:** olhando-me de cima para baixo • 6 **to straighten him out:** repreendê-lo

When I did nothing but return his gaze¹, he spoke, in an altered tone. "You see, Sergeant," he explained to me, "Friday nights, Jews are supposed to go to services."

"Did Sergeant Thurston tell you you couldn't go to them when there was a G.I. party?"

"No."

"Did he say you had to stay and scrub² the floors?"

"No, Sergeant."

"Did the Captain say you had to stay and scrub the floors?"

"That isn't it, Sergeant. It's the other guys in the barracks." He leaned toward me³. "They think we're goofing off⁴. But we're not. That's when Jews go to services, Friday night. We have to."

"Then go."

"But the other guys make accusations. They have no right."

"That's not the Army's problem, Grossbart. It's a personal problem you'll have to work out yourself."

"But it's un*fair*."

I got up to leave. "There's nothing I can do about it," I said. Grossbart stiffened⁵ and stood in front of me. "But this is a matter of *religion*, sir."

"Sergeant," I said.

"I mean 'Sergeant,'" he said, almost snarling⁶.

"Look, go see the chaplain⁷. You want to see Captain Barrett, I'll arrange an appointment."

"No, no. I don't want to make trouble, Sergeant. That's the first thing they throw up to you⁸. I just want my rights!"

---

1 **gaze:** olhar fixo • 2 **scrub:** esfregar • 3 **he leaned toward me:** se inclinou na minha direção • 4 **we're goofing off:** estamos brincando • 5 **stiffened:** enrijeceu • 6 **snarling:** rosnado • 7 **chaplain:** capelão • 8 **that's the first thing they throw up to you:** é a primeira coisa que jogam na sua cara

"Damn it, Grossbart, stop whining[1]. You have your rights. You can stay and scrub floors or you can go to shul[2] —"

The smile swam in again[3]. Spittle gleamed[4] at the corners of his mouth. "You mean church, Sergeant."

"I mean shul, Grossbart!"

I walked past him and went outside. Near me, I heard the scrunching of the guard's boots on gravel[5]. Beyond the lighted windows of the barracks, young men in T shirts and fatigue pants[6] were sitting on their bunks[7], polishing their rifles. Suddenly there was a light rustling[8] behind me. I turned and saw Grossbart's dark frame fleeing back to the barracks[9], racing to tell his Jewish friends that they were right — that, like Karl and Harpo, I was one of them.

The next morning, while chatting[10] with Captain Barrett, I recounted[11] the incident of the previous evening. Somehow, in the telling, it must have seemed to the Captain that I was not so much explaining Grossbart's position as defending it. "Marx, I'd fight side by side with a nigger if the fella[12] proved to me he was a man. I pride myself," he said, looking out the window, "that I've got an open mind. Consequently, Sergeant, nobody gets special treatment here, for the good *or* the bad. All a man's got to do is prove himself. A man fires well on the range[13], I give him a weekend pass. He scores high in

---

1 **stop whining:** pare de reclamar • 2 **shul:** sinagoga (em ídiche) • 3 **the smile swam in again:** o sorriso apareceu de novo • 4 **spittle gleamed:** a saliva brilhava • 5 **the scrunching of the guard's boots on gravel:** o raspar das botas do guarda no cascalho • 6 **fatigue pants:** roupas de trabalho • 7 **bunks:** beliches • 8 **a light rustling:** um leve farfalhar • 9 **Grossbart's dark frame fleeing back to the barracks:** a silhueta escura de Grossbart voltando à caserna • 10 **chatting:** conversava • 11 **recounted:** contei • 12 **fella:** companheiro • 13 **fires well on the range:** atira bem no campo

P.T.[1], he gets a weekend pass. He *earns* it." He turned from the window and pointed a finger at me. "You're a Jewish fella, am I right, Marx?"

"Yes, sir."

"And I admire you. I admire you because of the ribbons[2] on your chest. I judge a man by what he shows me on the field of battle, Sergeant. It's what he's got *here*," he said, and then, though I expected he would point to his heart, he jerked a thumb toward the buttons straining to hold his blouse across his belly[3]. "Guts[4]," he said.

"O.K., sir. I only wanted to pass on to you[5] how the men felt."

"Mr. Marx, you're going to be old before your time if you worry about how the men feel. Leave that stuff to the chaplain — that's his business, not yours. Let's us train these fellas to shoot straight[6]. If the Jewish personnel feels the other men are accusing them of goldbricking[7] — well, I just don't know. Seems awful funny[8] that suddenly the Lord is calling so loud in Private Grossman's ear he's just got to run to church."

"Synagogue," I said.

"Synagogue is right, Sergeant. I'll write that down for handy reference[9]. Thank you for stopping by[10]."

That evening, a few minutes before the company gathered[11] outside the orderly room for the chow formation[12], I called

---

1 **he scores high in P.T. (Physical Training):** se destaca no treinamento físico • 2 **ribbons:** condecorações • 3 **he jerked a thumb toward the buttons straining to hold his blouse across his belly:** mostrou com o polegar os botões que tentavam segurar a barriga dentro da camisa • 4 **guts:** tripas (expressão que indica coragem) • 5 **to pass on to you:** transmitir a você • 6 **to shoot straight:** atirar direito • 7 **goldbricking:** esquivar-se do serviço • 8 **awful funny:** muito curioso • 9 **handy reference:** referência prática • 10 **stopping by:** passar por aqui • 11 **gathered:** se juntar • 12 **chow formation:** fila da comida

the C.Q., Corporal Robert LaHill, in to see me. LaHill was a dark, burly fellow whose hair curled out of his clothes[1] wherever it could. He had a glaze[2] in his eyes that made one think of caves and dinosaurs. "LaHill," I said, "when you take the formation, remind the men that they're free to attend church services *whenever* they are held, provided they report to the orderly room before they leave the area."

LaHill scratched his wrist[3], but gave no indication that he'd heard or understood.

"LaHill," I said, "*church*. You remember? Church, priest, Mass[4], confession."

He curled one lip into a kind of smile[5]; I took it for a signal that for a second he had flickered back up into the human race[6].

"Jewish personnel who want to attend services this evening are to fall out[7] in front of the orderly room at 1900," I said. Then, as an afterthought, I added[8], "By order of Captain Barret."

A little while later, as the day's last light — softer than any I had seen that year — began to drop over[9] Camp Crowder, I heard LaHill's thick, inflectionless voice[10] outside my window: "Give me your ears, troopers. Toppie says for me to tell you that at 1900 hours all Jewish personnel is to fall out in front, here, if they want to attend the Jewish Mass."

---

1 **a dark, burly fellow whose hair curled out of his clothes:** um cara moreno e corpulento cujo pelo enrolado saía da roupa • 2 **glaze:** brilho transparente • 3 **scratched his wrist:** coçou seu pulso • 4 **mass:** missa • 5 **he curled one lip into a kind of smile:** ele curvou o lábio numa espécie de sorriso • 6 **he had flickered back up into the human race:** tinha voltado rapidamente para a condição humana • 7 **to fall out:** debandar • 8 **then, as an afterthought, I added:** em seguida, como me ocorreu, eu acrescentei • 9 **to drop over:** cair sobre • 10 **thick, inflectionless voice:** voz grave e monótona

DEFENDER OF THE FAITH

At seven o'clock, I looked out the orderly-room window and saw three soldiers in starched khakis[1] standing on the dusty quadrangle[2]. They looked at their watches and fidgeted[3] while they whispered back and forth. It was getting dimmer[4], and, alone on the otherwise deserted field, they looked tiny. When I opened the door, I heard the noises of the G.I. party coming from the surrounding barracks — bunks being pushed to the walls, faucets pounding water into buckets[5], brooms whisking[6] at the wooden floors, cleaning the dirt away for Saturday's inspection. Big puffs of cloth[7] moved round and round on the windowpanes[8]. I walked outside, and the moment my foot hit the ground I thought I heard Grossbart call to the others "'Ten-hut[9]!" Or maybe, when they all three jumped to attention, I imagined I heard the command.

Grossbart stepped forward, "Thank you, sir," he said.

"'Sergeant,' Grossbart," I reminded him. "You call officers 'sir.' I'm not an officer. You've been in the Army three weeks — you know that."

He turned his palms out at his sides[10] to indicate that, in truth, he and I lived beyond convention[11]. "Thank you, anyway," he said.

"Yes," a tall boy behind him said. "Thanks a lot."

And the third boy whispered, "Thank you," but his mouth

---

1 **starched khakis:** uniforme cáqui engomado • 2 **dusty quadrangle:** quadrilátero empoeirado • 3 **fidgeted:** se mexiam agitados • 4 **it was getting dimmer:** estava escurecendo • 5 **faucets pounding water into buckets:** torneiras derramando água em baldes • 6 **brooms whisking:** vassouras varrendo • 7 **puffs of cloth:** panos amassados • 8 **windowpanes:** vidros de janela • 9 **ten-hut!:** Sentido! (comando militar preparatório para outros comandos) • 10 **he turned his palms out at his sides:** virou as palmas da mão para fora • 11 **he and I lived beyond convention:** ele e eu estávamos além das convenções

barely fluttered¹, so that he did not alter by more than a lip's movement his posture of attention.

"For what?" I asked.

Grossbart snorted happily². "For the announcement. The Corporal's announcement. It helped. It made it —"

"Fancier³." The tall boy finished Grossbart's sentence.

Grossbart smiled. "He means formal, sir. Public," he said to me. "Now it won't seem as though we're just taking off⁴ — goldbricking because the work has begun."

"It was by order of Captain Barrett," I said.

"Aaah, but you pull a little weight⁵," Grossbart said. "So we thank you." Then he turned to his companions. "Sergeant Marx, I want you to meet Larry Fishbein."

The tall boy stepped forward⁶ and extended his hand. I shook it. "You from New York?" he asked.

"Yes."

"Me too." He had a cadaverous face that collapsed inward from his cheekbone to his jaw⁷, and when he smiled — as he did at the news of our communal attachment⁸ — revealed a mouthful of bad teeth. He was blinking his eyes a good deal⁹, as though he were fighting back tears. "What borough¹⁰?" he asked.

I turned to Grossbart. "It's five after seven. What time are services?"

"Shul," he said, smiling, "is in ten minutes. I want you to

---

1 **barely fluttered:** mal se mexeu • 2 **snorted happily:** bufou feliz • 3 **fancier:** mais bonito • 4 **we're just taking off:** simplesmente fugindo • 5 **you pull a little weight:** você que reforçou • 6 **stepped forward:** deu um passo adiante • 7 **that collapsed inward from his cheekbone to his jaw:** que se afundava desde a maçã do rosto até a mandíbula • 8 **communal attachment:** procedência comum • 9 **he was blinking his eyes a good deal:** ele piscava muito os olhos • 10 **borough:** distrito municipal

meet Mickey Halpern. This is Nathan Marx, our sergeant."

The third boy hopped forward[1]. "Private Michael Halpern." He saluted.

"Salute officers, Halpern," I said. The boy dropped his hand, and, on its way down, in his nervousness, checked to see if his shirt pockets were buttoned.

"Shall I march them over, sir[2]?" Grossbart asked. "Or are you coming along?"

From behind Grossbart, Fishbein piped up[3]. "Afterward, they're having refreshments. A ladies auxiliary from St. Louis, the rabbi told us last week."

"The chaplain," Halpern whispered.

"You're welcome to come along," Grossbart said.

To avoid his plea[4], I looked away, and saw, in the windows of the barracks, a cloud of faces staring out at the four of us. "Hurry along, Grossbart," I said.

"O.K., then," he said. He turned to the others. "Double time[5], *march*!" They started off, but ten feet away Grossbart spun around[6] and, running backward, called to me "Good *shabbus*[7], sir!" And then the three of them were swallowed into the alien Missouri dusk[8].

Even after they had disappeared over the parade ground[9], whose green was now a deep blue, I could hear Grossbart singing the double-time cadence, and as it grew dimmer and dimmer, it suddenly touched a deep memory — as did the

---

1 **hopped foward:** deu um pequeno salto para a frente • 2 **shall I march them over, sir?:** devo fazê-los marchar, senhor? • 3 **piped up:** levantou a voz • 4 **to avoid his plea:** para evitar seu apelo • 5 **double time:** acelerar o passo • 6 **spun around:** deu meia-volta • 7 **good shabbus!:** bom shabat! (o dia do descanso, sétimo dia da semana judaica) • 8 **were swallowed into the alien Missouri dusk:** foram engolidos pelo estranho anoitecer do Missouri • 9 **the parade ground:** praça de armas

slant of the light[1] — and I was remembering the shrill sounds[2] of a Bronx playground[3] where, years ago, beside the Grand Concourse[4], I had played on long spring evenings such as this. It was a pleasant memory for a young man so far from peace and home, and it brought so many recollections with it that I began to grow exceedingly tender about myself. In fact, I indulged myself in a reverie[5] so strong that I felt as though a hand were reaching down inside me. It had to reach so very far to touch me! It had to reach past those days in the forests of Belgium, and past the dying I'd refused to weep over[6]; past the nights in German farmhouses whose books we'd burned to warm us; past endless stretches[7] when I had shut off all softness I might feel for my fellows[8], and had managed even to deny myself the posture of a conqueror — the swagger[9] that I, as a Jew, might well have worn as my boots whacked against the rubble[10] of Wesel, Munster, and Braunschweig.

But now one night noise, one rumor of home and time past, and memory plunged down[11] through all I had anesthetized, and came to what I suddenly remembered was myself. So it was not altogether curious that, in search of more of me, I found myself following Grossbart's tracks to Chapel No. 3, where the Jewish services were being held.

I took a seat in the last row, which was empty. Two rows in front of me sat Grossbart, Fishbein, and Halpern, holding

---

1 **the slant of the light:** a inclinação da luz • 2 **shrill sounds:** sons estridentes • 3 **playground:** parquinho • 4 **Grand Concourse:** uma das principais ruas do Bronx • 5 **I indulged myself in a reverie:** eu me permiti um devaneio • 6 **to weep over:** chorar por • 7 **endless stretches:** distâncias intermináveis • 8 **I had shut off all softness I might feel for my fellows:** eu tinha bloqueado todo o afeto que eu pudesse sentir pelos meus companheiros • 9 **swagger:** vanglória • 10 **whacked against the rubble:** acertavam os escombros • 11 **plunged down:** mergulhou

DEFENDER OF THE FAITH 75

little white Dixie cups¹. Each row of seats was raised higher² than the one in front of it, and I could see clearly what was going on. Fishbein was pouring³ the contents of his cup into Grossbart's, and Grossbart looked mirthful⁴ as the liquid made a purple arc between Fishbein's hand and his. In the glaring⁵ yellow light, I saw the chaplain standing on the platform at the front; he was chanting⁶ the first line of the responsive reading. Grossbart's prayer book⁷ remained closed on his lap; he was swishing the cup around⁸. Only Halpern responded to the chant by praying. The fingers of his right hand were spread wide⁹ across the cover of his open book. His cap¹⁰ was pulled down low onto his brow¹¹, which made it round, like a yarmulke¹². From time to time, Grossbart wet his lips at the cup's edge; Fishbein, his long yellow face a dying light bulb¹³, looked from here to there, craning forward¹⁴ to catch sight of the faces down the row, then of those in front of him, then behind. He saw me, and his eyelids beat a tattoo¹⁵. His elbow slid into Grossbart's side, his neck inclined toward his friend, he whispered something, and then, when the congregation next responded to the chant, Grossbart's voice was among the others. Fishbein looked into his book now, too; his lips, however, didn't move.

Finally, it was time to drink the wine. The chaplain smiled down at them as Grossbart swigged¹⁶ his in one long

---

1 **Dixie cups:** copos de plástico • 2 **each row of seats was raised higher:** cada fileira de assentos era mais elevada • 3 **pouring:** vertendo • 4 **looked mirthful:** parecia alegre • 5 **glaring:** brilhante • 6 **chanting:** entoando • 7 **prayer book:** livro de orações • 8 **he was swishing the cup around:** fazia girar o vinho na taça • 9 **spread wide:** estendidos • 10 **cap:** quepe • 11 **brow:** têmpora • 12 **yarmulke:** quipá (pequeno chapéu de oração judaico em forma circular) • 13 **dying light bulb:** lâmpada fraca • 14 **craning forward:** esticando o pescoço para a frente • 15 **his eyelids beat a tattoo:** suas pálpebras bateram em retirada • 16 **swigged:** engoliu

gulp¹, Halpern sipped², meditating, and Fishbein faked devotion³ with an empty cup. "As I look down amongst the congregation"— the chaplain grinned⁴ at the word — "this night, I see many new faces, and I want to we come you to Friday-night services here at Camp Crowder. I am Major Leo Ben Ezra, your chaplain." Though an American, the chaplain spoke deliberately — syllable by syllable, almost — as though to communicate, above all, with the lip readers in his audience. "I have only a few words to say before we adjourn to the refreshment room⁵, where the kind ladies of the Temple Sinai, St. Louis, Missouri, have a nice setting for you."

Applause and whistling broke out. After another momentary grin, the chaplain raised his hands, palms out, his eyes flicking upward a moment, as if to remind the troops where they were and Who Else might be in attendance. In the sudden silence that followed, I thought I heard Grossbart cackle⁶, "Let the goyim⁷ clean the floors!" Were those the words? I wasn't sure, but Fishbein, grinning, nudged⁸ Halpern. Halpern looked dumbly⁹ at him, then went back to his prayer book, which had been occupying him all through the rabbi's talk. One hand tugged at the black kinky hair that stuck out under his cap¹⁰. His lips moved.

The rabbi continued. "It is about the food that I want to speak to you for a moment. I know, I know, I know," he in-

---

1 **one long gulp:** um gole longo • 2 **sipped:** bebericava • 3 **faked devotion:** fingia devoção • 4 **grinned:** sorriu • 5 **we adjourn to the refreshment room:** passemos ao salão (tipo de cafeteria) • 6 **cackle:** cacarejando • 7 **goyim:** os não judeus (no singular, gói) • 8 **nudged:** cutucou com o cotovelo • 9 **dumbly:** com cara de tonto • 10 **one hand tugged at the black kinky hair that stuck out under his cap:** uma mão puxava o cabelo preto e crespo que escapava de seu quepe

toned, wearily[1], "how in the mouths of most of you the *trafe* food[2] tastes like ashes. I know how you gag[3], some of you, and how your parents suffer to think of their children eating foods unclean and offensive to the palate. What can I tell you? I can only say, close your eyes and swallow as best you can. Eat what you must to live, and throw away the rest. I wish I could help more. For those of you who find this impossible, may I ask that you try and try, but then come to see me in private. If your revulsion is so great, we will have to seek aid from those higher up."

A round of chatter rose and subsided[4]. Then everyone sang "Ain Kelohainu[5]"; after all those years, I discovered I still knew the words. Then, suddenly, the service over, Grossbart was upon me. "Higher up? He means the General?"

"Hey, Shelly," Fishbein said, "he means God." He smacked his face[6] and looked at Halpern. "How high can you go!"

"Sh-h-h!" Grossbart said. "What do you think, Sergeant?"

"I don't know," I said. "You better ask the chaplain."

"I'm going to. I'm making an appointment to see him in private. So is Mickey."

Halpern shook his head. "No, no, Sheldon —"

"You have rights, Mickey," Grossbart said. "They can't push us around[7]."

"It's O.K.," said Halpern. "It bothers my mother, not me."

Grossbart looked at me. "Yesterday he threw up[8]. From the hash[9]. It was all ham and God knows what else."

1 **wearily:** exaustivamente • 2 ***trafe* food:** qualquer comida que não seja *kosher*, ou seja, proibida para judeus • 3 **you gag:** têm ânsia de vômito • 4 **a round of chatter rose and subsided:** uma rodada de murmúrios levantou-se e apaziguou-se • 5 **"Ain Kelohainu" (Ein Keloheinu):** hino judaico • 6 **he smacked his face:** deu-lhe uma bofetada • 7 **they can't push us around:** eles não podem nos forçar • 8 **he threw up:** ele vomitou • 9 **hash:** prato de carne e batata refogada

"I have a cold — that was why," Halpern said. He pushed his yarmulke back into a cap[1].

"What about you, Fishbein?" I asked. "You kosher[2], too?"

He flushed[3]. "A little. But I'll let it ride[4]. I have a very strong stomach, and I don't eat a lot anyway." I continued to look at him, and he held up his wrist to reinforce what he'd just said; his watch strap[5] was tightened to the last hole, and he pointed that out to me.

"But services are important to you?" I asked him.

He looked at Grossbart. "Sure, sir."

"'Sergeant.'"

"Not so much at home," said Grossbart, stepping between us, "but away from home it gives one a sense of his Jewishness."

"We have to stick together[6]," Fishbein said.

I started to walk toward the door; Halpern stepped back to make way for me.

"That's what happened in Germany," Grossbart was saying, loud enough for me to hear. "They didn't stick together. They let themselves get pushed around."

I turned. "Look, Grossbart. This is the Army, not summer camp."

He smiled. "So?" Halpern tried to sneak off[7], but Grossbart held his arm.

"Grossbart, how old are you?" I asked.

"Nineteen."

"And you?" I said to Fishbein.

"The same. The same month, even."

---

1 **he pushed his yarmulke back into a cap:** empurrou a quipá para trás como se fosse um quepe • 2 **kosher:** come apenas comida judaica • 3 **he flushed:** ruborizou • 4 **I'll let it ride:** vou deixar correr • 5 **watch strap:** tira do relógio • 6 **to stick together:** manter-nos unidos • 7 **to sneak off:** escapar

"And what about him?" I pointed to Halpern, who had by now made it safely to the door.

"Eighteen," Grossbart whispered. "But like he can't tie his shoes or brush his teeth himself. I feel sorry for him."

"I feel sorry for all of us, Grossbart," I said, "but just act like a man. Just don't overdo it[1]."

"Overdo what, sir?"

"The 'sir' business[2], for one thing. Don't overdo that," I said. I left him standing there. I passed by Halpern, but he did not look at me. Then I was outside, but, behind, I heard Grossbart call, "Hey, Mickey, my *leben*[3], come on back. Refreshments[4]!"

"*Leben!*" My grandmother's word for me!

One morning a week later, while I was working at my desk, Captain Barrett shouted for me to come into his office. When I entered, he had his helmet liner squashed down[5] so far on his head that I couldn't even see his eyes. He was on the phone, and when he spoke to me, he cupped one hand over the mouthpiece[6]. "Who the hell is Grossbart?"

"Third platoon, Captain," I said. "A trainee."

"What's all this stink[7] about food? His mother called a goddam congressman about the food." He uncovered the mouthpiece and slid his helmet up[8] until I could see his bottom eyelashes. "Yes, sir," he said into the phone. "Yes, sir. I'm still here, sir. I'm asking Marx, here, right now —"

---

1 **don't overdo it:** não exagere • 2 **the 'sir' business:** esse negócio de me chamar de "senhor" • 3 **my *leben*:** minha vida • 4 **refreshments:** refrescos; refeição rápida • 5 **squashed down:** enterrado • 6 **he cupped one hand over the mouthpiece:** ele cobria o bocal com a mão • 7 **stink:** porcaria • 8 **slid his helmet up:** levantou o capacete

He covered the mouthpiece again and turned his head back toward me. "Lightfoot Harry's on the phone," he said, between his teeth. "This congressman calls General Lyman, who calls Colonel Sousa, who calls the Major, who calls me. They're just dying to stick this thing on me[1]. Whatsa matter?" He shook the phone at me. "I don't feed the troops? What is this?"

"Sir, Grossbart is strange —" Barrett greeted that with a mockingly indulgent smile[2]. I altered my approach. "Captain, he's a very orthodox Jew, and so he's only allowed to eat certain foods."

"He throws up[3], the congressman said. Every time he eats something, his mother says, he throws up!"

"He's accustomed to observing the dietary laws, Captain."

"So why's his old lady have to call the White House?"

"Jewish parents, sir — they're apt[4] to be more protective than you expect. I mean, Jews have a very close family life. A boy goes away from home, sometimes the mother is liable to[5] get very upset. Probably the boy mentioned something in a letter, and his mother misinterpreted."

"I'd like to punch him one right in the mouth," the Captain said. "There's a goddam war on, and he wants a silver platter[6]!"

"I don't think the boy's to blame, sir. I'm sure we can straighten it out[7] by just asking him. Jewish parents worry —"

"*All* parents worry, for Christ's sake. But they don't get on their high horse[8] and start pulling strings[9] —"

---

1 **to stick this thing on me:** para jogar isso no meu colo • 2 **mockingly indulgent smile:** sorriso de escárnio, porém indulgente • 3 **he throws up:** vomita • 4 **apt:** propenso • 5 **is liable to:** é propensa a • 6 **silver platter:** bandeja de prata • 7 **straighten it out:** encontrar uma solução • 8 **they don't get on their high horse:** nem por isso são inflexíveis • 9 **start pulling strings:** começam a mexer os pauzinhos

I interrupted, my voice higher, tighter than before. "The home life, Captain, is very important — but you're right, it may sometimes get out of hand[1]. It's a very wonderful thing, Captain, but because it's so close, this kind of thing..."

He didn't listen any longer to my attempt to present both myself and Lightfoot Harry with an explanation for the letter. He turned back to the phone. "Sir?" he said. "Sir — Marx, here, tells me Jews have a tendency to be pushy[2]. He says he thinks we can settle it[3] right here in the company.... Yes, sir.... I will call back, sir, soon as I can." He hung up. "Where are the men, Sergeant?"

"On the range."

With a whack[4] on the top of his helmet, he crushed it down[5] over his eyes again, and charged out of his chair. "We're going for a ride," he said.

The Captain drove, and I sat beside him. It was a hot spring day, and under my newly starched fatigues[6] I felt as though my armpits were melting down[7] onto my sides and chest. The roads were dry, and by the time we reached the firing range, my teeth felt gritty[8] with dust, though my mouth had been shut the whole trip. The Captain slammed the brakes on[9] and told me to get the hell out and find Grossbart.

I found him on his belly, firing wildly at the five-hundred-feet target. Waiting their turns behind him were Halpern and Fishbein. Fishbein, wearing a pair of steel-rimmed G.I. glasses[10] I hadn't seen on him before, had the appearance of

---

1 **get out of hand:** sair do controle • 2 **pushy:** insistente • 3 **we can settle it:** podemos resolver • 4 **whack:** golpe • 5 **he crushed it down:** afundou-o • 6 **newly starched fatigues:** uniformes de campanha recém-engomados • 7 **as though my armpits were melting down:** como se minhas axilas estivessem derretendo • 8 **gritty:** arenosos • 9 **slammed the brakes on:** freou com tudo • 10 **steel-rimmed G.I. glasses:** óculos militares com armação de metal

an old peddler[1] who would gladly have sold you his rifle and the cartridges[2] that were slung all over him[3]. I stood back by the ammo boxes[4], waiting for Grossbart to finish spraying[5] the distant targets. Fishbein straggled back[6] to stand near me.

"Hello, Sergeant Marx," he said.

"How are you?" I mumbled.

"Fine, thank you. Sheldon's really a good shot."

"I didn't notice."

"I'm not so good, but I think I'm getting the hang of it[7] now. Sergeant, I don't mean to, you know, ask what I shouldn't —" The boy stopped. He was trying to speak intimately, but the noise of the shooting forced him to shout at me.

"What is it?" I asked. Down the range, I saw Captain Barrett standing up in the jeep, scanning the line[8] for me and Grossbart.

"My parents keep asking and asking where we're going," Fishbein said. "Everybody says the Pacific. I don't care, but my parents — if I could relieve their minds, I think I could concentrate more on my shooting."

"I don't know where, Fishbein. Try to concentrate anyway."

"Sheldon said you might be able to find out."

"I don't know a thing, Fishbein. You just take it easy, and don't let Sheldon —"

"*I'm* taking it easy, Sergeant. It's at home —"

Grossbart had just finished on the line, and was dusting his fatigues[9] with one hand. I called to him. "Grossbart, the Captain wants to see you."

---

1 **peddler:** vendedor ambulante • 2 **cartridges:** cartuchos • 3 **were slung all over him:** estavam pendurados em seu corpo • 4 **ammo boxes:** caixas de munição • 5 **spraying:** metralhar • 6 **straggled back:** demorou • 7 **I'm getting the hang of it:** estou pegando o jeito • 8 **scanning the line:** esquadrinhando a fila • 9 **dusting his fatigues:** tirando o pó do uniforme

He came toward us. His eyes blazed and twinkled[1]. "Hi!"

"Don't point that rifle!" I said.

"I wouldn't shoot you, Sarge." He gave me a smile as wide as a pumpkin[2], and turned the barrel aside[3].

"Damn you, Grossbart, this is no joke! Follow me."

I walked ahead of him, and had the awful suspicion that, behind me, Grossbart was *marching*, his rifle on his shoulder as though he were a one-man detachment[4]. At the jeep, he gave the Captain a rifle salute. "Private Sheldon Grossbart, sir."

"At ease[5], Grossman." The Captain sat down, slid over into the empty seat, and, crooking a finger, invited Grossbart closer[6].

"Bart, sir. Sheldon Gross*bart*. It's a common error." Grossbart nodded[7] at me; I understood, he indicated. I looked away just as the mess truck[8] pulled up to the range, disgorging[9] a half-dozen K.P.s[10] with rolled-up sleeves. The mess sergeant screamed at them while they set up the chow-line equipment[11].

"Grossbart, your mama wrote some congressman that we don't feed you right. Do you know that?" the Captain said.

"It was my father, sir. He wrote to Representative Franconi that my religion forbids me to eat certain foods."

"What religion is that, Grossbart?"

"Jewish."

" 'Jewish, *sir*,' " I said to Grossbart.

---

1 **his eyes blazed and twinkled:** seus olhos resplandeciam e cintilavam • 2 **wide as a pumpkin:** largo como uma abóbora • 3 **turned the barrel aside:** deixou o barril da arma de lado • 4 **one-man detachment:** destacamento militar de uma pessoa • 5 **at ease:** descansar (ordem militar) • 6 **crooking a finger, invited Grossbart closer:** com o dedo, convidou Grossbar a se aproximar • 7 **nodded:** assentiu com a cabeça • 8 **mess truck:** caminhão militar que leva a comida • 9 **disgorging:** desembarcando • 10 **K.P.'s (Kitchen Patrol):** soldados que trabalham na cozinha • 11 **while they set up the chow-line equipment:** enquanto instalavam o equipamento para a refeição

"Excuse me, sir. Jewish, sir."

"What have you been living on?" the Captain asked. "You've been in the Army a month already. You don't look to me like you're falling to pieces."

"I eat because I have to, sir. But Sergeant Marx will testify to the fact that I don't eat one mouthful more than I need to in order to survive."

"Is that so, Marx?" Barrett asked.

"I've never seen Grossbart eat, sir," I said.

"But you heard the rabbi," Grossbart said. "He told us what to do, and I listened."

The Captain looked at me. "Well, Marx?"

"I still don't know what he eats and doesn't eat, sir."

Grossbart raised his arms to plead with me[1], and it looked for a moment as though he were going to hand me his weapon to hold. "But, Sergeant —"

"Look, Grossbart, just answer the Captain's questions," I said sharply.

Barrett smiled at me, and I resented it[2]. "All right, Grossbart," he said. "What is it you want? The little piece of paper? You want out?"

"No, sir. Only to be allowed to live as a Jew. And for the others, too."

"What others?"

"Fishbein, sir, and Halpern."

"They don't like the way we serve, either?"

"Halpern throws up, sir. I've seen it."

"I thought *you* throw up."

"Just once, sir. I didn't know the sausage was sausage."

---

1 **to plead with me:** para me suplicar • 2 **I resented it:** eu me ressenti

DEFENDER OF THE FAITH

"We'll give menus, Grossbart. We'll show training films about the food, so you can identify when we're trying to poison you."

Grossbart did not answer. The men had been organized into two long chow lines[1]. At the tail end[2] of one, I spotted[3] Fishbein — or, rather, his glasses spotted me. They winked sunlight back at me[4]. Halpern stood next to him, patting[5] the inside of his collar with a khaki handkerchief. They moved with the line as it began to edge up toward the food[6]. The mess sergeant was still screaming at the K.P.s. For a moment, I was actually terrified by the thought that somehow the mess sergeant was going to become involved in Grossbart's problem.

"Marx," the Captain said, "you're a Jewish fella — am I right?"

I played straight man. "Yes, sir."

"How long you been in the Army? Tell this boy."

"Three years and two months."

"A year in combat, Grossbart. Twelve goddam months in combat all through Europe. I admire this man." The Captain snapped a wrist against my chest[7]. "Do you hear him peeping[8] about the food? Do you? I want an answer, Grossbart. Yes or no."

"No, sir."

"And why not? He's a Jewish fella."

"Some things are more important to some Jews than other things to other Jews."

---

1 **chow lines:** filas de soldados esperando pela refeição • 2 **tail end:** fim da fila • 3 **I spotted:** eu vi • 4 **they winked sunlight back at me:** o sol refletido neles me atingiu • 5 **patting:** secando (o suor) • 6 **to edge up toward the food:** aproximar-se lentamente da comida • 7 **snapped a wrist against my chest:** bateu o punho contra o meu peito • 8 **peeping:** reclamando

Barrett blew up[1]. "Look, Grossbart. Marx, here, is a good man — a goddam hero. When you were in high school, Sergeant Marx was killing Germans. Who does more for the Jews — you, by throwing up over a lousy[2] piece of sausage, a piece of first-cut meat[3], or Marx, by killing those Nazi bastards? If I was a Jew, Grossbart, I'd kiss this man's feet. He's a goddam hero, and *he* eats what we give him. Why do you have to cause trouble is what I want to know! What is it you're buckin' for — a discharge[4]?"

"No, sir."

"I'm talking to a wall! Sergeant, get him out of my way." Barrett swung himself back into the driver's seat[5]. "I'm going to see the chaplain." The engine roared, the jeep spun around in a whirl of dust[6], and the Captain was headed back to camp.

For a moment, Grossbart and I stood side by side, watching the jeep. Then he looked at me and said, "I don't want to start trouble. That's the first thing they toss up to us[7]."

When he spoke, I saw that his teeth were white and straight, and the sight of them suddenly made me understand that Grossbart actually did have parents — that once upon a time someone had taken little Sheldon to the dentist. He was their son. Despite all the talk about his parents, it was hard to believe in Grossbart as a child, an heir[8] — as related by blood to anyone, mother, father, or, above all, to me. This realization led me to another.

---

1 **blew up:** explodiu • 2 **lousy:** maldita • 3 **first-cut meat:** carne de primeira • 4 **what is it you are buckin' for — a discharge?:** o que você quer? Uma dispensa? • 5 **Barrett swung himself back into the driver's seat:** Barrett se jogou de volta ao banco do motorista • 6 **the jeep spun around in a whirl of dust:** o jipe fez a volta num redemoinho de poeira • 7 **they toss up to us:** jogam na nossa cara • 8 **an heir:** um herdeiro

"What does your father do, Grossbart?" I asked as we started to walk back toward the chow line.

"He's a tailor."

"An American?"

"Now, yes. A son in the Army," he said, jokingly.

"And your mother?" I asked.

He winked. "A *ballabusta*[1]. She practically sleeps with a dustcloth[2] in her hand."

"She's also an immigrant?"

"All she talks is Yiddish, still."

"And your father, too?"

"A little English. 'Clean,' 'Press,' 'Take the pants in.' That's the extent of it. But they're good to me."

"Then, Grossbart —" I reached out and stopped him. He turned toward me, and when our eyes met, his seemed to jump back, to shiver in their sockets[3]. "Grossbart — you were the one who wrote that letter, weren't you?"

It took only a second or two for his eyes to flash happy[4] again. "Yes." He walked on, and I kept pace[5]. "It's what my father *would* have written if he had known how. It was his name, though. *He* signed it. He even mailed it. I sent it home. For the New York postmark[6]."

I was astonished, and he saw it. With complete seriousness, he thrust[7] his right arm in front of me. "Blood is blood, Sergeant," he said, pinching the blue vein in his wrist[8].

"What the hell *are* you trying to do, Grossbart?" I asked.

---

1 **ballabusta:** dona de casa (termo ídiche) • 2 **dustcloth:** pano de limpeza • 3 **to shiver in their sockets:** tremer na base • 4 **it took only a second or two for his eyes to flash happy:** foi uma questão de segundos para que seus olhos brilhassem de felicidade • 5 **I kept pace:** segui seu ritmo • 6 **postmark:** carimbo do correio • 7 **he thrust:** enfiou • 8 **pinching the blue vein in his wrist:** beliscando a veia azul em seu pulso

"I've seen you eat. Do you know that? I told the Captain I don't know what you eat, but I've seen you eat like a hound[1] at chow."

"We work hard, Sergeant. We're in training. For a furnace to work, you've got to feed it coal[2]."

"Why did you say in the letter that you threw up all the time?"

"I was really talking about Mickey there. I was talking *for* him. He would never write, Sergeant, though I pleaded with him. He'll waste away[3] to nothing if I don't help. Sergeant, I used my name — my father's name — but it's Mickey, and Fishbein, too, I'm watching out for[4]."

"You're a regular Messiah, aren't you?"

We were at the chow line now.

"That's a good one, Sergeant," he said, smiling. "But who knows? Who can tell? Maybe you're the Messiah — a little bit. What Mickey says is the Messiah is a collective idea. He went to Yeshiva, Mickey, for a wile[5]. He says *together* we're the Messiah. Me a little bit, you a little bit. You should hear that kid talk, Sergeant, when he gets going."

"Me a little bit, you a little bit," I said. "You'd like to believe that, wouldn't you, Grossbart? That would make everything so clean for you."

"It doesn't seem too bad a thing to believe, Sergeant. It only means we should all give a little, is all."

I walked off to eat my rations with the other noncoms[6].

---

1 **eat like a hound:** devorar a comida • 2 **for a furnace to work, you've got to feed it coal:** para que a caldeira funcione, você tem que botar carvão • 3 **he'll waste away:** ele vai definhar • 4 **I'm watching out for:** estou preocupado • 5 **wile:** artimanha • 6 **noncoms:** suboficiais

Two days later, a letter addressed to Captain Barrett passed over my desk. It had come through the chain of command[1] — from the office of Congressman Franconi, where it had been received, to General Lyman, to Colonel Sousa, to Major Lamont, now to Captain Barrett. I read it over twice. It was dated May 14, the day Barrett had spoken with Grossbart on the rifle range.

Dear Congressman:

First let me thank you for your interest in behalf of my son, Private Sheldon Grossbart. Fortunately, I was able to speak with Sheldon on the phone the other night, and I think I've been able to solve our problem. He is, as I mentioned in my last letter, a very religious boy, and it was only with the greatest difficulty that I could persuade him that the religious thing to do — what God Himself would want Sheldon to do — would be to suffer the pangs of religious remorse[2] for the good of his country and all mankind[3]. It took some doing[4], Congressman, but finally he saw the light. In fact, what he said (and I wrote down the words on a scratch pad[5] so as never to forget), what he said was "I guess you're right, Dad. So many millions of my fellow-Jews gave up their lives to the enemy, the least I can do is live for a while minus a bit of my heritage so as to help end this struggle[6] and regain for all the children of God dignity and humanity." That, Congressman, would make any father proud.

By the way, Sheldon wanted me to know — and to pass on to you — the name of a soldier who helped him reach this decision:

---

1 **chain of command:** cadeia de comando • 2 **to suffer the pangs of religious remorse:** sofrer os tormentos do remorso religioso • 3 **mankind:** humanidade • 4 **it took some doing:** foi trabalhoso • 5 **scratch pad:** bloco de notas • 6 **struggle:** luta

SERGEANT NATHAN MARX. Sergeant Marx is a combat veteran who is Sheldon's first sergeant. This man has helped Sheldon over some of the first hurdles[1] he's had to face in the Army, and is in part responsible for Sheldon's changing his mind about the dietary laws. I know Sheldon would appreciate any recognition Marx could receive.

Thank you and good luck. I look forward to seeing your name on the next election ballot[2].

> Respectfully,
> Samuel E. Grossbart

Attached to the Grossbart communiqué was another, addressed to General Marshall Lyman, the post commander, and signed by Representative Charles E. Franconi, of the House of Representatives[3]. The communiqué informed General Lyman that Sergeant Nathan Marx was a credit to the U.S. Army and the Jewish people.

What was Grossbart's motive in recanting[4]? Did he feel he'd gone too far? Was the letter a strategic retreat — a crafty[5] attempt to strengthen what he considered our alliance? Or had he actually changed his mind, via an imaginary dialogue between Grossbart *père* and Grossbart *fils*? I was puzzled, but only for a few days — that is, only until I realized that, whatever his reasons, he had actually decided to disappear from my life; he was going to allow himself to become just another trainee. I saw him at inspection, but he never winked; at chow formations, but he never flashed me a sign. On Sundays, with the other trainees, he would sit around watching the noncoms'

---

1 **hurdles:** obstáculos • 2 **ballot:** cédula • 3 **House of Representatives:** Câmara de Representantes (equivalente à Câmara dos Deputados) • 4 **recanting:** retratar-se • 5 **crafty:** hábil

softball[1] team, for which I pitched[2], but not once did he speak an unnecessary word to me. Fishbein and Halpern retreated, too — at Grossbart's command, I was sure. Apparently he had seen that wisdom lay in turning back before he plunged over into the ugliness of privilege undeserved[3]. Our separation allowed me to forgive him our past encounters, and, finally, to admire him for his good sense.

Meanwhile, free of Grossbart, I grew used to my job and my administrative tasks. I stepped on a scale[4] one day, and discovered I had truly become a noncombatant; I had gained seven pounds. I found patience to get past the first three pages of a book. I thought about the future more and more, and wrote letters to girls I'd known before the war. I even got a few answers. I sent away to Columbia for a Law School catalogue. I continued to follow the war in the Pacific, but it was not my war. I thought I could see the end, and sometimes, at night, I dreamed that I was walking on the streets of Manhattan — Broadway, Third Avenue, 116th Street, where I had lived the three years I attended Columbia. I curled myself around[5] these dreams and I began to be happy.

And then, one Sunday, when everybody was away and I was alone in the orderly room reading a month-old copy of the *Sporting News*[6], Grossbart reappeared.

"You a baseball fan, Sergeant?"

I looked up. "How are you?"

---

1 **softball:** esporte similar ao beisebol que se joga com uma bola um pouco maior • 2 **for which I pitched:** no qual eu jogava como lançador (*pitcher*) • 3 **wisdom lay in turning back before he plunged over into the ugliness of privilege undeserved:** a sabedoria consistia em voltar atrás antes de mergulhar na indignidade do privilégio não merecido • 4 **I stepped on a scale:** subi em uma balança • 5 **I curled myself around:** me envolvi em • 6 *Sporting News*: revista norte-americana especializada em beisebol

"Fine," Grossbart said. "They're making a soldier out of me."

"How are Fishbein and Halpern?"

"Coming along," he said. "We've got no training this afternoon. They're at the movies."

"How come[1] you're not with them?"

"I wanted to come over and say hello."

He smiled — a shy, regular-guy smile, as though he and I well knew that our friendship drew its sustenance[2] from unexpected visits, remembered birthdays, and borrowed lawnmowers[3]. At first it offended me, and then the feeling was swallowed by the general uneasiness[4] I felt at the thought that everyone on the post was locked away in a dark movie theater and I was here alone with Grossbart. I folded up my paper.

"Sergeant," he said, "I'd like to ask a favor. It is a favor, and I'm making no bones about it[5]."

He stopped, allowing me to refuse him a hearing[6] — which, of course, forced me into a courtesy I did not intend. "Go ahead."

"Well, actually, it's two favors."

I said nothing.

"The first one's about these rumors. Everybody says we're going to the Pacific."

"As I told your friend Fishbein, I don't know," I said. "You'll just have to wait to find out. Like everybody else."

"You think there's a chance of any of us going East?"

"Germany?" I said. "Maybe."

"I meant New York."

---

1 **how come...?:** por quê...? • 2 **drew its sustenance:** se alimentava • 3 **borrowed lawnmowers:** cortadores de grama emprestados • 4 **uneasiness:** inquietação • 5 **I'm making no bones about it:** vou ser direto e reto • 6 **allowing me to refuse him a hearing:** para permitir que eu me recusasse a ouvi-lo

"I don't think so, Grossbart. Offhand[1]."

"Thanks for the information, Sergeant," he said.

"It's not information, Grossbart. Just what I surmise[2]."

"It certainly would be good to be near home. My parents — you know." He took a step toward the door and then turned back. "Oh, the other thing. May I ask the other?"

"What is it?"

"The other thing is — I've got relatives in St. Louis, and they say they'll give me a whole Passover[3] dinner if I can get down there. God, Sergeant, that'd mean an awful lot to me."

I stood up. "No passes during basic[4], Grossbart."

"But we're off from now till Monday morning, Sergeant. I could leave the post and no one would even know."

"I'd know. You'd know."

"But that's all. Just the two of us. Last night, I called my aunt, and you should have heard her. 'Come — come,' she said. 'I got gefilte fish[5], *chrain*[6] — the works[7]!' Just a day, Sergeant. I'd take the blame if anything happened."

"The Captain isn't here to sign a pass."

"You could sign."

"Look, Grossbart —"

"Sergeant, for two months, practically, I've been eating *trafe* till I want to die."

"I thought you'd made up your mind[8] to live with it. To be minus a little bit of heritage."

---

1 **offhand:** a princípio • 2 **what I surmise:** o que eu suponho • 3 **Passover:** Páscoa judaica (comemora a saída do povo judeu do Egito) • 4 **no passes during basic:** não há folgas no período de instrução básica • 5 **gefilte fish:** bolinho de peixe cozido (prato judaico típico) • 6 ***chrain:*** pasta de raiz-forte • 7 **the works!:** tenho de tudo! • 8 **I thought you'd made up your mind:** pensei que você já tinha decidido

He pointed a finger at me. "You!" he said. "That wasn't for you to read."

"I read it. So what?"

"The letter was addressed to a congressman."

"Grossbart, don't feed me any baloney[1]. You *wanted* me to read it."

"Why are you persecuting me, Sergeant?"

"Are you kidding!"

"I've run into this before," he said, "but never from my own!"

"Get out of here, Grossbart! Get the hell out of my sight!"

He did not move. "Ashamed, that's what you are," he said. "So you take it out on the rest of us[2]. They say Hitler himself was half a Jew. Hearing you, I wouldn't doubt it."

"What are you trying to do with me, Grossbart?" I asked him. "What are you after[3]? You want me to give you special privileges, to change the food, to find out about your orders, to give you weekend passes."

"You even talk like a goy!" Grossbart shook his fist. "Is this just a weekend pass I'm asking for? Is a Seder[4] sacred, or not?"

Seder! It suddenly occurred to me that Passover had been celebrated weeks before. I said so.

"That's right," he replied. "Who says no? A month ago — and I was in the field eating hash! And now all I ask is a simple favor. A Jewish boy I thought would understand. My aunt's willing to go out of her way[5] — to make a Seder a month

---

1 **don't feed me any baloney:** não me venha com essa • 2 **so you take it out on the rest of us:** então você desconta em nós • 3 **what are you after?:** o qu e você quer? • 4 **Seder:** ceia celebrada na primeira noite da páscoa judaica • 5 **willing to go out of her way:** disposta a se dar ao trabalho

later...." He turned to go, mumbling.

"Come back here!" I called. He stopped and looked at me. "Grossbart, why can't you be like the rest? Why do you have to stick out like a sore thumb[1]?"

"Because I'm a Jew, Sergeant. I *am* different. Better, maybe not. But different."

"This is a war, Grossbart. For the time being *be* the same."

"I refuse."

"What?"

"I refuse. I can't stop being me, that's all there is to it[2]." Tears came to his eyes. "It's a hard thing to be a Jew. But now I understand what Mickey says — it's a harder thing to stay one." He raised a hand sadly toward me. "Look at *you*."

"Stop crying!"

"Stop this, stop that, stop the other thing! You stop, Sergeant. Stop closing your heart to your own!" And, wiping his face with his sleeve[3], he ran out the door. "The least[4] we can do for one another — the least..."

An hour later, looking out of the window, I saw Grossbart headed across the field. He wore a pair of starched khakis and carried a little leather ditty bag[5]. I went out into the heat of the day. It was quiet; not a soul was in sight except, over by the mess hall, four K.P.s sitting around a pan[6], sloped forward from their waists[7], gabbing[8] and peeling potatoes in the sun.

"Grossbart!" I called.

---

1 **to stick out like a sore thumb:** se fazer notar como um dedo ferido (expressão que significa "ser diferente de todos") • 2 **that's all there is to it:** isso é tudo • 3 **wiping his face with his sleeve:** limpando o rosto com a manga • 4 **the least:** o mínimo • 5 **leather ditty bag:** pequena bolsa de viagem de couro • 6 **pan:** panela • 7 **sloped forward from the waist:** inclinados para a frente • 8 **gabbing:** conversando

He looked toward me and continued walking.

"Grossbart, get over here!"

He turned and came across the field. Finally, he stood before me.

"Where are you going?" I asked.

"St. Louis. I don't care."

"You'll get caught without a pass."

"So I'll get caught without a pass."

"You'll go to the stockade[1]."

"I'm *in* the stockade." He made an about-face and headed off[2]. I let him go only a step or two. "Come back here," I said, and he followed me into the office, where I typed out a pass and signed the Captain's name, and my own initials after it.

He took the pass and then, a moment later, reached out and grabbed my hand. "Sergeant, you don't know how much this means to me."

"O.K.," I said. "Don't get in any trouble."

"I wish I could show you how much this means to me."

"Don't do me any favors. Don't write any more congressmen for citations."

He smiled. "You're right. I won't. But let me do something."

"Bring me a piece of that gefilte fish. Just get out of here."

"I will!" he said. "With a slice of carrot and a little horseradish[3]. I won't forget."

"All right. Just show your pass at the gate. And don't tell *anybody*."

"I won't. It's a month late, but a good Yom Tov[4] to you."

---

1 **stockade:** prisão militar • 2 **he made an about-face and headed off:** deu meia-volta e foi embora • 3 **horseradish:** raiz-forte • 4 **Yom Tov:** feriado (em ídiche)

"Good Yom Tov, Grossbart," I said.

"You're a good Jew, Sergeant. You like to think you have a hard heart, but underneath you're a fine, decent man. I mean that."

Those last three words touched me more than any words from Grossbart's mouth had the right to. "All right, Grossbart," I said. "Now call me 'sir,' and get the hell out of here."

He ran out the door and was gone. I felt very pleased with myself; it was a great relief to stop fighting Grossbart, and it had cost me nothing. Barrett would never find out, and if he did, I could manage to invent some excuse. For a while, I sat at my desk, comfortable in my decision. Then the screen door flew back and Grossbart burst in[1] again. "Sergeant!" he said. Behind him I saw Fishbein and Halpern, both in starched khakis, both carrying ditty bags like Grossbart's.

"Sergeant, I caught Mickey and Larry coming out of the movies. I almost missed them."

"Grossbart — did I say to tell no one?" I said.

"But my aunt said I could bring friends. That I should, in fact."

"*I'm* the Sergeant, Grossbart — not your aunt!"

Grossbart looked at me in disbelief. He pulled Halpern up by his sleeve. "Mickey, tell the Sergeant what this would mean to you."

Halpern looked at me and, shrugging, said. "A lot."

Fishbein stepped forward without prompting[2]. "This would mean a great deal to me and my parents, Sergeant Marx."

"No!" I shouted.

---

1 **burst in:** entrou bruscamente • 2 **without prompting:** sem ser chamado

Grossbart was shaking his head[1]. "Sergeant, I could see you denying me, but how can you deny Mickey, a Yeshiva boy — that's beyond me."

"I'm not denying Mickey anything," I said. "You just pushed a little too hard, Grossbart. *You* denied him."

"I'll give him my pass, then," Grossbart said. "I'll give him my aunt's address and a little note. At least let him go."

In a second, he had crammed[2] the pass into Halpern's pants pocket. Halpern looked at me, and so did Fishbein. Grossbart was at the door, pushing it open. "Mickey, bring me a piece of gefilte fish, at least," he said, and then he was outside again.

The three of us looked at one another, and then I said, "Halpern, hand that pass over[3]."

He took it from his pocket and gave it to me. Fishbein had now moved to the doorway, where he lingered[4]. He stood there for a moment with his mouth slightly open, and then he pointed to himself. "And me?" he asked.

His utter ridiculousness exhausted me. I slumped down in my seat[5] and felt pulses knocking at the back of my eyes. "Fishbein," I said, "you understand I'm not trying to deny you anything, don't you? If it was my Army, I'd serve gefilte fish in the mess hall. I'd sell *kugel*[6] in the PX[7], honest to God."

Halpern smiled.

"You understand, don't you, Halpern?"

"Yes, Sergeant."

"And you, Fishbein? I don't want enemies. I'm just like

---

1 **shaking his head:** negando com a cabeça • 2 **he had crammed:** ele tinha enfiado • 3 **hand that pass over:** me devolva esse passe • 4 **where he lingered:** onde ele permaneceu • 5 **I slumped down in my seat:** me afundei na cadeira • 6 ***kugel*:** prato tradicional judaico e alemão semelhante a uma torta • 7 **PX (store):** lojas que funcionam em bases militares

you — I want to serve my time and go home. I miss the same things you miss."

"Then, Sergeant," Fishbein said, "why don't you come, too?"

"Where?"

"To St. Louis. To Shelly's aunt. We'll have a regular Seder. Play hide-the-matzoh[1]." He gave me a broad, black-toothed smile.

I saw Grossbart again, on the other side of the screen.

"Pst!" He waved[2] a piece of paper. "Mickey, here's the address. Tell her I couldn't get away."

Halpern did not move. He looked at me, and I saw the shrug[3] moving up his arms into his shoulders again. I took the cover off my typewriter and made out passes for him and Fishbein. "Go," I said. "The three of you."

I thought Halpern was going to kiss my hand.

That afternoon, in a bar in Joplin, I drank beer and listened with half an ear to the Cardinal game[4]. I tried to look squarely[5] at what I'd become involved in, and began to wonder if perhaps the struggle with Grossbart wasn't as much my fault as his. What was I that I had to *muster*[6] generous feelings? Who was I to have been feeling so grudging, so tight-hearted[7]? After all, I wasn't being asked to move the world. Had I a right, then, or a reason, to clamp down[8] on Grossbart, when that meant clamping down on Halpern, too? And Fishbein

---

1 **hide-the-matzoh:** ritual típico da Páscoa judaica que consiste em esconder a matzá (pão ázimo) para as crianças buscarem • 2 **he waved:** agitou • 3 **shrug:** encolhimento • 4 **the Cardinal game:** jogo do Cardinals (time de beisebol de St. Louis) • 5 **squarely:** diretamente • 6 **to muster:** reunir (também significa "passar em revista") • 7 **so grudging, so tight-hearted:** tão relutante, tão duro • 8 **to clamp down:** tomar medidas mais drásticas

— that ugly, agreeable soul[1]? Out of the many recollections of my childhood that had tumbled over me[2] these past few days I heard my grandmother's voice: "What are you making a *tsimmes*[3]?" It was what she would ask my mother when, say, I had cut myself while doing something I shouldn't have done, and her daughter was busy bawling me out[4]. I needed a hug and a kiss, and my mother would moralize. But my grandmother knew — mercy overrides justice[5]. I should have known it, too. Who was Nathan Marx to be such a penny pincher[6] with kindness? Surely, I thought, the Messiah himself — if He should ever come — won't niggle over nickels and dimes[7]. God willing[8], he'll hug and kiss.

The next day, while I was playing softball over on the parade ground, I decided to ask Bob Wright, who was noncom in charge of Classification and Assignment, where he thought our trainees would be sent when their cycle ended, in two weeks. I asked casually, between innings[9], and he said, "They're pushing them all into the Pacific. Shulman cut the orders on your boys the other day."

The news shocked me, as though I were the father of Halpern, Fishbein, and Grossbart.

That night, I was just sliding into sleep[10] when someone tapped[11] on my door. "Who is it?" I asked.

"Sheldon."

---

1 **agreeable soul:** alma cândida • 2 **that had tumbled over me:** que caíram sobre mim • 3 ***tsimmes*:** confusão (em ídiche) • 4 **bawling me out:** me repreendendo • 5 **mercy overrides justice:** a compaixão sobrepuja a justiça • 6 **penny pincher:** avarento • 7 **won't niggle over nickels and dimes:** não se preocupará com coisas pequenas • 8 **God willing:** se Deus quiser • 9 **innings:** entre uma entrada e outra no jogo de beisebol • 10 **I was just sliding into sleep:** eu estava pegando no sono • 11 **tapped:** bateu levemente

He opened the door and came in. For a moment, I felt his presence without being able to see him. "How was it?" I asked.

He popped into sight[1] in the near-darkness before me. "Great, Sergeant." Then he was sitting on the edge of the bed. I sat up.

"How about you?" he asked. "Have a nice weekend?"

"Yes."

"The others went to sleep." He took a deep, paternal breath. We sat silent for a while, and a homey feeling[2] invaded my ugly little cubicle; the door was locked, the cat was out, the children were safely in bed.

"Sergeant, can I tell you something? Personal?"

I did not answer, and he seemed to know why. "Not about me. About Mickey. Sergeant, I never felt for anybody like I feel for him. Last night I heard Mickey in the bed next to me. He was crying so, it could have broken your heart. Real sobs[3]."

"I'm sorry to hear that."

"I had to talk to him to stop him. He held my hand, Sergeant — he wouldn't let it go. He was almost hysterical. He kept saying if he only knew where we were going. Even if he knew it *was* the Pacific, that would be better than nothing. Just to know."

Long ago, someone had taught Grossbart the sad rule that only lies can get the truth. Not that I couldn't believe in the fact of Halpern's crying; his eyes *always* seemed red-rimmed[4]. But, fact or not, it became a lie when Grossbart uttered it[5].

1 **he popped into sight:** apareceu de repente • 2 **homey feeling:** sensação de lar • 3 **real sobs:** soluços verdadeiros • 4 **red-rimmed:** avermelhados • 5 **uttered it:** dizia

He was entirely strategic. But then — it came with the force of indictment[1] — so was I! There are strategies of aggression, but there are strategies of retreat[2] as well. And so, recognizing that I myself had not been without craft and guile[3], I told him what I knew. "It is the Pacific."

He let out a small gasp[4], which was not a lie. "I'll tell him. I wish it was otherwise[5]."

"So do I."

He jumped on my words. "You mean you think you could do something? A change, maybe?"

"No, I couldn't do a thing."

"Don't you know anybody over at C. and A.[6]?"

"Grossbart, there's nothing I can do," I said. "If your orders are for the Pacific, then it's the Pacific."

"But Mickey —"

"Mickey, you, me — everybody, Grossbart. There's nothing to be done. "Maybe the war'll end before you go. Pray for a miracle."

"But —"

"Good night, Grossbart." I settled back, and was relieved to feel the springs unbend[7] as Grossbart rose to leave. I could see him clearly now; his jaw had dropped, and he looked like a dazed prizefighter[8]. I noticed for the first time a little paper bag in his hand.

"Grossbart." I smiled. "My gift?"

"Oh, yes, Sergeant. Here — from all of us." He handed me the bag. "It's egg roll[9]."

---

1 **indictment:** acusação (figurado) • 2 **retreat:** retirada • 3 **craft and guile:** artimanhas • 4 **gasp:** grito contido • 5 **otherwise:** de outra forma • 6 **C. and A. (Commission and Assignment):** escritório de missões e nomeações • 7 **to feel the springs unbend:** sentir as molas da cama voltarem ao lugar • 8 **a dazed prizefighter:** um boxeador atordoado • 9 **egg roll:** rolinho primavera

"Egg roll?" I accepted the bag and felt a damp grease spot[1] on the bottom. I opened it, sure that Grossbart was joking.

"We thought you'd probably like it. You know — Chinese egg roll. We thought you'd probably have a taste for[2] —"

"Your aunt served egg roll?"

"She wasn't home."

"Grossbart, she invited you. You told me she invited you and your friends."

"I know," he said. "I just reread the letter. *Next* week."

I got out of bed and walked to the window. "Grossbart," I said. But I was not calling to him.

"What?"

"What are you, Grossbart? Honest to God, what are you?"

I think it was the first time I'd asked him a question for which he didn't have an immediate answer.

"How can you do this to people?" I went on.

"Sergeant, the day away did us all a world of good. Fishbein, you should see him, he *loves* Chinese food."

"But the Seder," I said.

"We took second best[3], Sergeant."

Rage came charging at me[4]. I didn't sidestep[5]. "Grossbart, you're a liar!" I said. "You're a schemer[6] and a crook[7]. You've got no respect for anything. Nothing at all. Not for me, the truth — not even for poor Halpern! You use us all —"

"Sergeant, Sergeant, I feel for Mickey. Honest to God, I do. I *love* Mickey. I try —"

---

1 **a damp grease spot:** uma mancha úmida e gordurosa • 2 **you'd probably have a taste for:** que provavelmente você gostasse disso • 3 **we took second best:** nos conformamos com a segunda melhor opção • 4 **rage came charging at me:** a raiva tomou conta de mim • 5 **I didn't sidestep:** não a evitei • 6 **schemer:** maquinador de planos • 7 **crook:** trapaceiro

"You try! You feel!" I lurched toward him[1] and grabbed his shirt front[2]. I shook him furiously. "Grossbart, get out! Get out and stay the hell away from me. Because if I see you, I'll make your life miserable. *You understand that?*"

"Yes."

I let him free[3], and when he walked from the room, I wanted to spit[4] on the floor where he had stood. I couldn't stop the fury. It engulfed me, owned me[5], till it seemed I could only rid myself of it[6] with tears or an act of violence. I snatched[7] from the bed the bag Grossbart had given me and, with all my strength, threw it out the window. And the next morning, as the men policed[8] the area around the barracks, I heard a great cry go up from one of the trainees, who had been anticipating only his morning handful of cigarette butts[9] and candy wrappers[10]. "Egg roll!" he shouted. "Holy Christ, Chinese goddam egg roll!"

A week later, when I read the orders that had come down from C. and A., I couldn't believe my eyes. Every single trainee was to be shipped[11] to Camp Stoneman, California, and from there to the Pacific — every trainee but one. Private Sheldon Grossbart. He was to be sent to Fort Monmouth, New Jersey. I read the mimeographed sheet several times. Dee, Farrell, Fishbein, Fuselli, Fylypowycz, Glinicki, Gromke, Gucwa, Halpern, Hardy, Helebrandt, right down to Anton Zygadlo

---

1 **I lurched toward him:** avancei cambaleando sobre ele • 2 **grabbed his shirt front:** agarrei sua camisa pela frente • 3 **I let him free:** eu o soltei • 4 **to spit:** cuspir • 5 **it engulfed me, owned me:** me envolvia, tomava conta de mim • 6 **rid myself of it:** livrar-me dela • 7 **I snatched:** agarrei • 8 **policed:** patrulhavam • 9 **cigarrete butts:** bitucas de cigarro • 10 **candy wrappers:** papéis de bala • 11 **was to be shipped:** ia embarcar

— all were to be headed West before the month was out. All except Grossbart. He had pulled a string[1], and I wasn't it.

I lifted the phone and called C. and A.

The voice on the other end said smartly, "Corporal Shulman, sir."

"Let me speak to Sergeant Wright."

"Who is this calling, sir?"

"Sergeant Marx."

And, to my surprise, the voice said, "*Oh!*" Then, "Just a minute, Sergeant."

Shulman's "*Oh!*" stayed with me while I waited for Wright to come to the phone. Why "*Oh!*"? Who was Shulman? And then, so simply, I knew I'd discovered the string that Grossbart had pulled. In fact, I could hear Grossbart the day he'd discovered Shulman in the PX, or in the bowling alley, or maybe even at services. "Glad to meet you. Where you from? Bronx? Me, too. Do you know So-and-So? And So-and-So? Me, too! You work at C. and A.? Really? Hey, how's chances of getting East? Could you do something? Change something? Swindle[2], cheat[3], lie? We gotta help each other, you know. If the Jews in Germany..."

Bob Wright answered the phone. "How are you, Nate? How's the pitching arm[4]?"

"Good. Bob, I wonder if you could do me a favor." I heard clearly my own words, and they so reminded me of Grossbart that I dropped more easily than I could have imagined into what I had planned. "This may sound crazy, Bob, but I got a kid here on orders to Monmouth who wants them changed.

---

1 **he had pulled a string:** tinha mexido os pauzinhos • 2 **swindle:** enganar • 3 **cheat:** trapacear • 4 **the pitching arm:** o braço de lançador (no beisebol)

He had a brother killed in Europe, and he's hot to go to the Pacific. Says he'd feel like a coward if he wound up Stateside[1]. I don't know, Bob — can anything be done? Put somebody else in the Monmouth slot[2]?"

"Who?" he asked cagily[3].

"Anybody. First guy in the alphabet. I don't care. The kid just asked if something could be done."

"What's his name?"

"Grossbart, Sheldon."

Wright didn't answer.

"Yeah," I said. "He's a Jewish kid, so he thought I could help him out. You know."

"I guess I can do something," he finally said. "The Major hasn't been around for weeks. Temporary duty to the golf course[4]. I'll try, Nate, that's all I can say."

"I'd appreciate it, Bob. See you Sunday." And I hung up[5], perspiring[6].

The following day, the corrected orders appeared: Fishbein, Fuselli, Fylypowycz, Glinicki, Gromke, Grossbart, Gucwa, Halpern, Hardy... Lucky Private Harley Alton was to go to Fort Monmouth, New Jersey, where, for some reason or other, they wanted an enlisted man with infantry training.

After chow that night, I stopped back at the orderly room to straighten out the guard-duty roster[7]. Grossbart was waiting for me. He spoke first.

"You son of a bitch!"

---

1 **if wound up Stateside:** acabar ficando no país (Estados Unidos) • 2 **slot:** posto • 3 **cagily:** cautelosamente • 4 **temporary duty to the golf course:** missão temporária no campo de golfe • 5 **I hung up:** desliguei o telefone • 6 **perspiring:** suando • 7 **to straigthen out the guard-duty roster:** para organizar os turnos de guarda

I sat down at my desk, and while he glared at me[1], I began to make the necessary alterations in the duty roster.

"What do you have against me?" he cried. "Against my family? Would it kill you for me to be near my father, God knows how many months he has left to him?"

"Why so?"

"His heart," Grossbart said. "He hasn't had enough troubles in a lifetime, you've got to add to them. I curse[2] the day I ever met you, Marx! Shulman told me what happened over there. There's no limit to your anti-Semitism, is there? The damage you've done here isn't enough. You have to make a special phone call! You really want me dead!"

I made the last notations in the duty roster and got up to leave. "Good night, Grossbart."

"You owe me an explanation!" He stood in my path.

"Sheldon, you're the one who owes explanations."

He scowled[3]. "To *you*?"

"To me, I think so — yes. Mostly[4] to Fishbein and Halpern."

"That's right, twist things around[5]. I owe nobody nothing. I've done all I could for them. Now I think I've got the right to watch out for myself."

"For each other we have to learn to watch out, Sheldon. You told me yourself."

"You call this watching out for me — what you did?"

"No. For all of us."

---

1 **while he glared at me:** enquanto me olhava fixamente • 2 **I curse:** eu amaldiçoo • 3 **he scowled:** ele franziu a testa • 4 **mostly:** principalmente • 5 **twist things around:** inverter as coisas

I pushed him aside and started for the door. I heard his furious breathing behind me, and it sounded like steam rushing from an engine of terrible strength[1].

"*You'll* be all right," I said from the door. And, I thought, so would Fishbein and Halpern be all right, even in the Pacific, if only Grossbart continued to see — in the obsequiousness[2] of the one, the soft spirituality of the other — some profit for himself.

I stood outside the orderly room, and I heard Grossbart weeping[3] behind me. Over in the barracks, in the lighted windows, I could see the boys in their T shirts sitting on their bunks talking about their orders, as they'd been doing for the past two days. With a kind of quiet nervousness, they polished shoes, shined belt buckles[4], squared away underwear[5], trying as best they could to accept their fate[6]. Behind me, Grossbart swallowed hard, accepting his. And then, resisting with all my will an impulse to turn and seek pardon for my vindictiveness[7], I accepted my own.

---

1 **like steam rushing from an engine of terrible strength:** como o vapor expelido de um motor de extrema potência • 2 **obsequiousness:** subserviência • 3 **weeping:** chorando • 4 **shined belt buckles:** lustravam as fivelas dos seus cintos • 5 **squared away underwear:** dobravam e guardavam a roupa de baixo • 6 **fate:** destino • 7 **vindictiveness:** espírito vingativo